My Story

WAR NURSE

Sue Reid

■ SCHOLASTIC

For Andrea

While the events described and some of the characters in this book may
be based on actual historical events and real people, Kitty Langley
is a fictional character, created by the author, and her diary
is a work of fiction.

Scholastic Children's Books
Euston House, 24 Eversholt Street,
London, NW1 1DB, UK
A division of Scholastic Ltd
London ~ New York ~ Toronto ~ Sydney ~ Auckland
Mexico City ~ New Delhi ~ Hong Kong

First published in the UK by Scholastic Ltd, 2005
This edition published 2009

ISBN 978 1407 10867 4

Standhaven Military Hospital, 1939

Sunday 3 September 1939

We were all at home when the news came. It was an ordinary Sunday – just like any other Sunday in our family.

Mother was closeted in the kitchen with Cook. Father ambled out of his study, paper in one hand, pipe clamped between his teeth. Peter was bent over the wireless, fiddling with the controls. Peter's my brother, two years older and a bit of a whizz with gadgets – at least he thinks he is. I told him to stop or we'd miss the Prime Minister's broadcast – and then he told me we would anyway if he couldn't fix it and we had a bit of an argy-bargy about it.

Then at 11.15 exactly – as if by magic – the crackles stopped and the Prime Minister's sombre voice drifted into the room. Mother and Cook rushed out of the kitchen. Father slowly put down his paper and took the pipe out of his mouth.

Five minutes – that's all it took to turn our world upside down.

We were at war with Germany. That's what the Prime Minister had told us.

Deep down I don't think any of us were surprised. Under their leader, Adolf Hitler, the Germans had already marched into Austria and Czechoslovakia. Then two days ago they'd invaded Poland. This time Hitler was given an ultimatum. If he didn't agree to withdraw his army from Poland by eleven o'clock this morning, a state of war would exist between our two countries. He hadn't.

I sat there, as if frozen. Peter's hands were motionless on the controls. Suddenly, I found myself wishing that we hadn't quarrelled. Then I heard a click as he leaned across and switched the wireless off. Somehow that seemed to wake us up again.

Mother got up first. "I'll help you pack, Kitten," she said, practical as ever. I got to my feet too then.

A week ago, I'd had a letter from the Red Cross. It said I was to report to Standhaven Military Hospital as soon as war was declared. I'd joined the Red Cross as soon as it seemed likely there'd be a war. I wanted to be a VAD – a Red Cross nurse. (We're called VADs after the Voluntary Aid Detachments which we're all members of.) Even though I'd been at school most of the time I'd managed to pass my First Aid and Home Nursing exams *and* complete my training in our local hospital. Now I'm allowed to nurse soldiers.

In my bedroom, I dragged my suitcase out from under the bed. The last time I'd packed it I'd been going back to school. All that was behind me now. But it still made me feel a bit odd.

There was a lot to go in. First, my VAD uniform.

I opened the wardrobe, where the uniform hung, and laid it out on the bed. There was an awful lot of it. Some of it – like the navy serge overcoat – I wouldn't need until winter. Then there was my nurse's uniform. Carefully I folded the grey-blue dresses and the white aprons with the big red cross on the bib. Then there were the white half-sleeves that I wear on top of my nurse's dress, and caps to go in too. When everything was packed, I put on my "outdoor" uniform – a navy serge jacket and skirt, worn with a white shirt and black tie, black cotton stockings and rubber-soled clumpy black shoes (horrid!).

Mother pinned a badge on to my sleeve. She looked terribly proud as she did it. That badge says that I'm a "mobile VAD", which means that I can be posted to an army hospital anywhere in the country. When I'm 21 – in two years' time – I'll even be able to serve abroad.

Last of all, I put on the hat. Peter roared with laughter when he saw me in it. He said I looked as if I had a pudding basin upside down on my head. "We army chaps had better look out!" he said. I felt annoyed and opened my mouth to tick him off, when something made me stop.

"We army chaps," he'd said. Only then did it dawn on me. I'd be nursing young men – boys – like him.

It could even be *my* brother, lying wounded, in bed. Suddenly I felt so frightened. Peter was joining the Infantry. He looked so young – far too young to be going off to fight.

"Oh, Peter," I gasped suddenly. I flung my arms round him, burrowing my head into his shoulder, not wanting him to see that my eyes were wet. He hugged me back and then he stuck a finger under my chin and looked down into my face, all big-brotherly.

"Don't be a goose, Sis," he said, fishing in his pocket for a hanky. "I'll be all right. You'll see."

Then the phone rang. It was Anne – my best friend. Like me she'd joined the Red Cross and we'd done our training together. Unlike me, she was still waiting to be called up.

"I rang to tell you the news," she said.

"I know. War. Isn't it awful?"

There was silence down the line. Something was wrong. "I'm not coming with you," she said. She went on in a rush before I could say anything. "I've been posted to an army hospital – near Leeds! I can't think why!" She gave that throaty laugh of hers. I felt too choked to speak. When I didn't say anything Anne went on: "Kitten, look. I'm going to keep a diary. Will you keep one too? We can pretend we're writing to each other. When it's all over we can show them to each other."

"Why don't we just write to each other?" I said tearfully.

"The post's bound to be awful, Father says. It'll be fun," she urged when I didn't answer. "I will write to you too of course."

"Promise?"

"Promise."

"All right then," I said slowly, even though I wasn't sure how I felt about showing my diary to anyone – even Anne. A diary is a private thing.

And then the line crackled and Mother called to me and so sadly I said goodbye and put the phone down. Everything in my life was changing – and all of it horrid.

The rest of the morning passed in a bit of a whirl. Somehow the news had leaked out that we were off and soon it felt as if the entire village was trooping into the house. Peter and I were made to parade up and down the drawing room in our uniforms. I felt awfully embarrassed but Peter looked wonderful in his lieutenant's uniform.

Peter left first – everyone being terribly brave about it – and then it was my turn. Bert, our gardener and odd-job man, helped us pack up the car. "What have you got in here, miss?" he gasped as he heaved my suitcase into the boot. Then there was my bicycle and tennis racket – even my hockey stick – to fit in.

"Honestly, Mother, I'm not going back to school!" I

protested when I saw her march up to the car with *that*, but she said you never know, it may come in handy. I don't know how we got it all in.

As we drove away I turned back. It all looked so safe and cosy, the house nestling amongst the trees, Cook and Bert standing by the door, waving.

I felt as if I was losing something precious and my eyes grew watery again. I tried to pull myself together.

The old life was over, I told myself – but the new one was about to begin. It would be an adventure.

Truth to tell, I was feeling lonely and a bit frightened. We were at war and I was going away – far away from everyone I cared about. Already I felt homesick. Who would I talk to when things were bad? Who could I tell about how I felt?

Then Anne's words floated into my mind. Her voice in my head was as clear as if she was in the car with me.

"I'm going to keep a diary. Will you keep one too?"

I haven't kept a diary since I was a child.

I'd promised her I'd do this.

I needed a friend – a friend I could say *anything* to. Maybe my diary will be that friend for me?

I was dropped off at the station. From there I had to catch a train down to the hospital.

On the platform there were a lot of girls and young

women, all wearing the same uniform as me. Some of the older ones had stripes on their jackets, which told me that they'd been VADs for far longer than me. I scanned their faces, but I couldn't see anyone I knew. Where were the girls who'd trained with me?

We VADs weren't the only people waiting for the train. As I skulked on the platform, a soldier winked at me.

"Going back to school, miss?" he asked. He was grinning as he looked at my hockey stick. I blushed hotly. "None of your lip, Private," a Sergeant told him sternly.

The train drew up with a whistle and great puff of steam. Suddenly the Sergeant was by my side.

"We'll help you with that, miss." He jerked his finger at a group of soldiers. "Oy, you. Over here."

I stood back, feeling a bit dazed as the soldiers swarmed around us, heaving suitcases, rackets and bicycles up on to the train.

Inside my compartment I studied the faces opposite me. We smiled shyly at each other from under our pudding-basin hats. We didn't know each other now, but one day, I told myself, those faces would be almost as familiar to me as my own.

3 September, 11 o'clock pm

I'm writing this under the bedclothes, my diary on my knees, torch in one hand, pencil in the other. I can't turn on the light or I might wake Nurse Mason. And in any case, there's the blackout to think about.

I've not been at the hospital for one whole day, but already I've so much to write about.

I'll begin with the hospital. It's a sprawling Victorian building, rather like St Jude's, my old school. As we drove through the grounds in the bus the army sent to meet us, I saw green lawns and tennis courts and then the hospital itself came into view, slipping in and out behind the trees.

Our sleeping quarters are in the hospital itself. Most of us are in dormitories, but I'm billeted in a small room on the second floor. I share it with one other nurse. All I know about her is that her name is Nurse Mason – and unlike me she's very tidy; there's not one thing out of place on the boxes we use as our dressing table and cupboards. I don't know how she's going to cope with sharing with me, or me with her.

The only other thing there's room for in here are our beds.

My bed's awful. First of all it's tiny so that if I stretch out in it my legs hang over the end. Then there's the mattress – a horrid lumpy thing that Bunty says is called "army biscuits". I thought she was joking but Marjorie and Molly say it's true and their father's a colonel so they should know. But when you look out of the window, you can see trees and through them a scrap of shimmering silver – the sea. That almost makes up for everything else.

After we'd been dropped off we were told to assemble in the hall. Matron and a QA Sister were going to talk to us. Mostly it seemed to be about what they expected of us – and what we could expect of them.

The QAs are members of Queen Alexandra's Imperial Military Nursing Service. They're our superiors, for – unlike us – they're fully trained professional nurses. The Regular QAs are full-time army nurses. The Reserves are civilian nurses who joined up when war broke out, like us.

Last of all we had a talk from a Sergeant, who reeled off a lot of stuff that I just know I'll have trouble remembering. Army rules – there seem to be so many of them.

There's one other important person I should mention. This is the Commandant. She calls us "Members" and we call her "Madam". The Commandant's a sort of chief VAD, and she looks awfully fierce. But she says we're to go to her if ever we have a problem.

After they'd gone, I was standing in the hall feeling a bit lost and lonely again when suddenly I heard a shriek. "Kitten!"

I blushed pink. Now everyone would know my nickname!

And then I saw who it was weaving through the packed hall towards me.

"Bunty!" I cried. "Bunty!" I flew across the room and hugged her. "Where were you? I didn't see you on the train."

"Mother dropped me and the twins off," she told me. I looked up at the two girls who'd followed her across the room. They grinned at me.

"Molly! Marjorie!" I cried, hugging each of them.

"Isn't this fun," said Bunty, beaming. "The old St Jude's gang – together again."

"Where's Anne?" Molly asked me. "Didn't she come on the train with you?"

"No," I said dolefully. "The army's sent her to Leeds."

"How absolutely typical!" said Marjorie.

"But why? She joined the same detachment as us!" exclaimed Molly.

"Never mind," said Bunty, hugging me again. "You've got us."

After our "medicals" – all us new VADs have to have these – and supper in the VADs' dining room (the army calls this a "mess"!) we piled into my tiny room. I dived into my luggage, scattering stuff everywhere, hunting for my chocolates – Mother's farewell present.

"Your mother's such a darling," Bunty said, mouth full. "Remind me never to eat a meal in the hospital again."

"It wasn't that bad," said Marjorie.

Just then the door opened and we all looked round. A tall, thin girl was standing in the doorway. I saw her stare at us, all squashed up on the bed together. My eyes followed hers round the room. It was an awful mess. I went pink.

"Hello," I said. "I'm Kitty Langley – you must be my roommate, Nurse Mason." I smiled and held out the chocolates. "I'm sorry about the mess," I added hastily.

She didn't smile back. She just stared at the chocolates – as if she'd never seen one before. Most peculiar.

"No, thank you," she said stiffly at last.

The door closed quietly behind her. We all stared at it.

"Not very friendly," Bunty said.

"She's probably just shy," said Molly kindly.

I shrugged. It probably wasn't going to be much fun sharing with Nurse Mason, but just then I had more important things on my mind.

Tomorrow I begin work – on a medical ward. I'm longing to start though I feel awfully nervous too, but Molly's on duty with me. That's something.

Monday 4 September

I was already awake when my alarm went at six. I had a crick in my neck from the hard army bolster, but I was too excited to care. It was my very first day as a military nurse.

I stumbled about in the semi-darkness, fumbling with the buttons on my uniform, hunting for my white sleeves and apron, while my roommate opened the blackout shutters.

I couldn't do my cap at all!

I raced down the corridor to the dorm. "Bunty!" I wailed, putting my head round the door. Bunty was still in bed.

"Go away," she mumbled.

"It's half past six!" I said, but she just groaned and pulled the sheet up over her head. I couldn't see the twins.

No time to lose. I tore back to my room. I looked at the rectangle of starched white cloth in despair – already it was crumpled from all my attempts to fold the wretched thing.

I felt like bursting into tears. My very first morning and I was going to be late.

Nurse Mason came to my rescue. "Give it to me," she said. I was so surprised that I just handed it to her. I watched as she laid the rumpled rectangle out on the bed, smoothed out the creases and expertly folded it – three neat pleats on each side. Then she pinned it on my head.

"Thank you," I mumbled, feeling awfully small. The merest glimmer of a smile flickered across my roommate's pale face.

I watched as she carefully pinned on her own cap. Unlike me, of course, she'd remembered to make it up the night before. She patted her hair. Not that she needed to – there wasn't a single strand out of place under the crease-free cap.

I just do not know what to make of Nurse Mason!

After breakfast I made my way down to the medical ward where I was to work – Ward B. I was feeling very nervous as I walked down the long corridor, my rubber-soled shoes noiseless on the lino. I'd already got lost once. Outside a pair of double doors, I stopped. Taking a deep breath, I pushed them open.

Before you reach the ward you have to pass Sister's office. There's a window in the office, so that the Sisters can look into the ward and see everything that's going on. Not that our Sister needs it, though – Sister Rook has eyes in the back of her head.

Beyond the office stretches the ward proper – two long rows of beds, one down each side of the room. I counted twenty – ten on each side – but quite a few of the beds were empty. There were screens leaning against the wall. These are pulled round the patients' beds when they need some privacy – like when they're being given a bedbath, or having a dressing changed. Most of the patients were sitting up in bed, bowls of water and shaving foam in front of them. Two men dressed identically in shapeless blue suits – the hospital "blues" worn by all patients allowed up – were playing cards at the ward table.

I'd arrived on the ward punctually at 7.30. Another VAD was already there. It was Nurse Mason.

There was one other person in Sister's office. A pair of beady eyes looked up at me from under a QA's long, flowing cap. "Another raw VAD," they seemed to say. "What *am* I to do with them?"

At 7.35 Molly appeared. I listened as she stammered out her explanation. She'd got lost, she said. Found herself on the Surgical ward. Was sent down here. Sister nodded, as if she'd heard it all before.

"All my girls know that I will not tolerate lateness," said Sister Rook severely, when we were all assembled. Her gaze rested on Molly. I felt my toes curl inside my shoes. It could so easily have been me.

She took us through our duties. "We have our own ways

of doing things here," Sister said. This, I was soon to learn, fell far short of the truth.

Top of Sister's list was cleanliness. "I expect the ward to be thoroughly cleaned. I will not tolerate dust. It's dirty and spreads disease," she announced.

The beady eyes rested on us again, as if daring us to contradict her.

"Yes, Sister," we chorused.

Untidiness was next on Sister's list. She looked at me as if she'd guessed how untidy I am. I blushed. Wish I didn't blush so easily.

Trolleys were being wheeled into the ward now, and Nurse Mason and I were sent off to give the patients their breakfast.

"Nurse Smythe, I'd like a word with you," I heard Sister say to Molly as Nurse Mason and I scuttled off. As I went from bed to bed, trying not to spill the sloppy porridge, I saw Molly shoot past us into the annexe at the end of the ward. When she came out again her eyelids were pink. I wondered what Sister had said to her. I did feel sorry for Molly then.

After the patients had finished, we darted round the beds again, removing bowls and mugs. One of the men sitting at the table winked at me – I smiled at him, hoping he couldn't tell how nervous I was feeling.

Next we had to do the cleaning. There's an awful lot

of it – and we VADs have to do it all – every day. I was quite surprised when I discovered this. In the civilian hospital where I'd done my training the cleaning was done by wardmaids. In a military hospital, Molly told me, it's usually done by orderlies of the Royal Army Medical Corps (RAMC). But most of ours have gone out to France.

Before we could start we had to pull out all the beds – awfully heavy, as most had patients still in them. After that out came all the lockers.

Now we had to sweep up all the fluff.

I went over to the annexe where I'd been told the cleaning things were kept. I looked around helplessly. Over by the wall, I could see an odd long-handled thing and a large tin of polish. I couldn't see anything else.

I poked my head out of the annexe. Sister was nowhere to be seen.

Very well then – I'd improvise. I ran some water into a sink – it was cold. Again I searched for a mop – but all I could find were some old rags. Was I supposed to use *them*?

"Nurse Langley!"

I jumped.

"This is *not* how we do the cleaning. Oh dear me, no!" Sister sighed impatiently and opened a tall cupboard. I already knew it was empty, but I didn't dare say so. Sister stared into the empty cupboard in disbelief.

Did she apologize? Oh no! "Run along," was all she said abruptly.

Run *where*?

"Be quick about it," she added. "Medical Officer's round at nine."

The "MO" was the doctor, I knew. I ran.

Somehow I managed to scrounge what we needed, and up and down that ward we went again, first one side, then the other, sweeping up the dust and blanket fluff. Then we had to polish the floor using the long-handled thing – it's called a "bumper".

All the time we were doing this the patients egged us on: "That's it, miss, you've got a very good swing there, miss. . . Wish I had muscles like you, miss." My cheeks were flaming now, and it wasn't just the exertion.

Now for the locker tops. After I'd scrubbed the first one thoroughly, I began to put the patient's things back inside.

"Not like that," cried Sister. The army had its own way of doing this, I discovered – even the patients' clothes and wash things have to be laid out in a certain way.

As I carefully folded the clothes in the way I'd been shown, Sister walked by clucking, "Hurry up, Nurse Langley, we don't have all day."

My arms were aching, my back hurt – and I was sure that Sister Rook had it in for me. The patients had gone very quiet but I felt that they were on my side.

We still had the polishing to do. All the brass needed a good shine, apparently – every tiny bit of it – even doorknobs, bed castors and keyholes! Sister says this is very important, but I can't understand why. Neither can Molly, and when Sister was out of earshot (chatting on the wards is *not* allowed) we had a bit of a grumble about it.

It was nine o'clock. Time for the Medical Officer's round. I was standing at the foot of a patient's bed when the MO entered the ward with Sister. He must have walked past me at least twice on his round – and each time I swear he looked straight through me, as if I didn't exist. Sister was hanging on his every word. It was all "Yes, Major", "No, Major" as they went round the ward together. But he's a *doctor*, I thought, puzzled. Why did Sister address Dr Roberts as "Major" – it wasn't as if he was a soldier? Later, Molly explained. "The doctors and surgeons here are all in the RAMC. They have military ranks, just like soldiers in the army." Honestly, there's just so much to remember!

At ten o'clock my first shift ended and I was sent off for my break. At one I was back on the ward and then I was on duty again until eight. By that time I was so tired that all I wanted to do was crawl out of the ward on my hands and knees.

One of our QA Staff Nurses – Nurse Winter – smiled at

me as I left. "You poor kid," she said sympathetically. "Your first day and the worst shift of all."

It *was* the worst shift I thought, as I made my way back along the corridor. We VADs get a three-hour break during the day. Molly was lucky – hers was at five – so she'd already finished for the day. I made my way into the VADs' "mess" for supper.

I slid into my seat. Nurse Mason was there, but I couldn't see Bunty or the twins. As I picked tiredly at my food – corned beef and potatoes again – I wondered where they were. I wanted to find out how they'd got on today – our first day on the wards. I wondered if they felt like me – too tired to know what I felt. Nurse Mason looked tired too. She gave me a tiny smile, but I don't think either of us said a word through the whole meal.

Tuesday 5 September

On Ward B Sister's eye is on us constantly, and if *she's* not hovering, it's Matron. Sister Rook treats us as if we know absolutely nothing. All our Red Cross training – it doesn't seem to count for anything here. It's almost as if we've never even *been* on a ward before.

And then there are the patients. These are sick soldiers who've been sent to us from forces billeted in the area. Sick *officers* are nursed separately in their own block. None of the soldiers have been in action yet. Many of them don't look any older than Peter, and some of them are such teases.

They've already given us nicknames. They're really cheeky. I've not discovered what mine is yet. To my face it's always "miss" – never "nurse".

They like to play jokes on us too. And today it was my turn.

I'd just slapped polish on the floor and was struggling to get the bumper moving when I heard a hoarse voice behind me.

"Miss, I'd like a bedbath."

It was Private Porter. "Now, Private, you know this isn't the time for your bath," I said, trying to sound both firm and sympathetic at the same time.

"Oh, please, miss," he said. "I spilt me tea all down meself."

I had a lot to do before the MO's round and Private Porter's a large man. I did *not* want to stop and give him a bedbath. I did not have *time* to give him a bedbath. But I had no choice.

"I'll just see what the damage is," I said, trying to sound cheerful. Dutifully I marched over to the screens and began to pull one of them over to the Private's bed.

The screen was big and heavy, and it wobbled dangerously as I hauled it across the ward. I was just going back for another one, when I heard a second voice call plaintively: "Miss! Miss!"

This patient wanted a bedbath too!

"Me too, miss." I whirled round again.

This patient was sitting, fully dressed, at the ward table. As I looked at him, he shut one brown eye in a long, slow wink. Only then did I realize that they were teasing me! I felt such an idiot.

Unfortunately for me, Sister had heard all the fuss. "What's going on here?" she asked, bustling into the ward. "Well?" she said, looking at Molly, Nurse Mason and me in turn. "Nurse Langley – I should have known," her face seemed to say, as her eyes rested on my scarlet face. I stuttered out an explanation.

"Private Porter wants a bedbath."

"It's not time for his bath," she said, eyebrows raised.

"I . . . I know, Sister," I said feebly. "He says he spilt his tea. I . . . I mean. . ." I didn't know what to say. How could I tell Sister that they'd been teasing me?

"Hmph," she said, and I saw her vanish behind the screen by the Private's bed.

I don't know what went on behind the screen, but Private Porter didn't say anything more about a bedbath after that.

Me, I returned to the bumpering. I seized the handle in both hands. I'll show them, I thought furiously. I'll show them that I can do something well. Ward B's floor was going to get the best polish it had ever had. Slowly I heaved the bumper back and forth, puffing from the effort. Suddenly I found that it was gliding easily over the floor. I turned to find a pair of strong male hands gripping the handle next to mine.

"Sorry about that, miss," the Private murmured. "We didn't mean to get you into trouble with Sister."

Whispering, he told me that his name was Private Barrett and then he asked *my* name. He looked sad when I just said "Nurse Langley". We're not allowed to tell the patients our first names. It's another hospital rule and *not* to be broken. Not ever.

Wednesday 6 September

This morning Nurse Winter showed us how to sterilize the instruments. Dressing bowls, forceps, bandages, scissors – everything has to be sterilized to prevent our patients from picking up infections. We have two sterilizers for this on Ward B. One for all the instruments, the other for dressing bowls. Things like bandages and dressings are sterilized in the autoclave in the operating-theatre suite.

After Nurse Winter had shown us what to do, we all had a go – Nurse Mason, Molly and me.

When it was my turn, I scrubbed my hands thoroughly – our hands have to be spotlessly clean too! – and then I lifted the lid of one of the sterilizers and popped in the instruments. When it had done its job, I lifted the lid again, pulled down the handle and watched the water drain away.

Then we watched as Nurse Winter whisked a pair of forceps out of a jar of disinfectant. "Cheatle forceps," I murmured, looking at the long-handled scissor-like instrument with the curved blades.

Nurse Winter looked at me. "Quite right, Nurse Langley. Can you tell me what we use them for?"

I could!

"To pick up other sterile objects – like swabs or other instruments," I said automatically.

"Would you do that for me now?"

I took the pair of forceps and carefully plucked out each instrument from the sterilizer in turn, tipping the surplus fluid back inside. One by one I placed each item on to the dressing tray.

"Thank you, Nurse Langley," she said when I'd finished.

"You did that very well." It was only a little thing but I did feel pleased.

On the notice board this afternoon, BIG warning. Colonel's inspection in the morning. Before we went off duty, Sister told us just how important this is. The Colonel's the most senior-ranking doctor in the hospital. We're all on our toes!

Thursday 7 September

Today was my first Colonel's inspection. What a to-do it is – and to think we get put through this every week!

Everything had to be absolutely spotless. *I* thought we already did a thorough job, but this morning I found out what a clean ward really is. The "up" patients lent us a hand, but even with their help, it was a rush to get everything done in time. Five minutes before the Colonel was due, my reddened hands squeaky clean, fresh apron donned, I scurried back into the ward. In front of me, one of our "up" patients ambled slowly across the room to his bed.

Ash was spilling off the end of his cigarette on to the

sparkling linoleum. The Colonel would have our guts for this, I thought, despairingly.

A man with bristly ginger hair hauled himself up in bed.

"What do you think you're doing, Private Barrett?" Corporal Smart wheezed.

"Corporal!" Private Barrett leapt to attention.

"Colonel's inspection, you dozy soldier!"

"Corporal!"

"At eleven!"

"Corporal!"

"So jump to it, soldier!"

Private Barrett stubbed out his cigarette in the tin hat dangling on the locker by his bed. At that Corporal Smart's face turned puce! Private Barrett winked at me, and loped off to clean up the mess, the tin hat swinging in his hand.

At eleven o'clock on the dot the big ward doors swung open and in walked the Colonel, escorted by Matron and what seemed to me to be half the hospital staff. The "up" patients stood stiffly to attention in front of their beds. As the Colonel entered, an order rang out and they clicked their heels smartly together. I felt as if I was on parade – not in a hospital ward at all.

I watched as the Colonel stopped at each patient's bedside; he was listening intently to Matron, but I could tell that he'd miss nothing. I looked round the ward, feeling almost too scared to breathe. The floor shone, but was it really clean? Each bedstead gleamed, but had we polished them thoroughly enough? Each shiny bed castor was lined up with the one next to it. Our sickest patients lay very still under the smoothed-down sheets – they looked almost as scared as me.

The Colonel stopped and ran a white-gloved hand over a locker. We all drew in breath together. The Colonel turned his gloved hand over and inspected it.

My heart began to thump. Almost I felt as if it was *me* who was being inspected.

The glove was spotless, and the Colonel walked on again. It seemed we'd passed – this time.

Friday 8 September

Private Barrett was discharged back to his regiment this morning. I was sent to the store to get his kit and take back his hospital "blues".

"Goodbye, Kitten," he whispered slyly to me as he left. I went beet red. How *did* Private Barrett find out my nickname?

Today we got our first week's pay. For this we all had to line up at Company Office and one by one we were given our wages.

"Langley," barked a voice when it was my turn. I stepped forward and something was pressed into my hand. I looked down. £1 didn't seem a lot for all our hard work, but it was the first money I'd ever earned and I felt quite proud. Not everyone felt the same it seemed, for as we were walking away, I heard a VAD say in a piercing voice, "Oh, I could *never* manage on *this*! *So* lucky that I don't have to." I wished she'd stop banging on about it. Not everyone has parents rich enough to send them an allowance. Nurse Mason was standing nearby. Her face was absolutely stony.

Saturday 9 September

So lucky – my half day off and the others are off too! Slept in – bliss! – and then we cycled into town together – Bunty, me, Molly and Marjorie. I asked Nurse Mason if she'd like to come too, but I was quite relieved when she said no thank you, she had a lot to do. I raced along to the dorm, where the others were waiting for me. It was heaven to get away from the hospital and we sang as we cycled along.

It was very quiet in the town. Because it's on the coast, a lot of the townspeople have left and many of the houses – and a lot of the shops – are boarded up.

After cycling around for a time, we found an ice cream parlour that was still open, and Bunty treated us all to strawberry ice cream. Delish!

We ate our ices sitting on the beach and then I lay back on the warm sand, pillowing my head on my arms.

"So – what's the verdict?" A shadow fell across my face and I opened my eyes to find Bunty peering at me.

I shut my eyes again. I didn't feel like talking.

"Come on, Kitten – tell," Bunty wheedled. "I want to know all about Ward B."

"Ask Molly," I said sleepily.

"Is it true that Sister Rook is the most terrifying QA in the hospital?"

"No," said Marjorie. "That's Sister Brown."

"Who's she?" I asked, eyes still shut.

"She's the Sister on *my* ward," said Marjorie.

We giggled and I sat up, hugging my knees.

"I think I'm lucky then," said Bunty. "Sister Bolton on my ward is sweet."

"How are you getting on with Nurse Mason, Kitty?" asked Marjorie.

"She's all right," I said. "But I wish I was in the dorm with all of you."

"Kitten," said Bunty firmly. "I want to know. Do you like being an army nurse?"

"It's all cleaning, bedbaths and bedpans," I said. "I'd like to do some *real* nursing."

"You and your real nursing," said Bunty. "You're a VAD, not a trained nurse."

"I know, I know," I said, lying back down again. I knew that Bunty was right, but still, I wanted to do more. *Proper* nursing. We cycled slowly back, along the promenade that runs above the beach. While the others rode on ahead I stopped for a moment and stared out to sea. It was another glorious autumn day and the sea looked so calm and peaceful, yet somewhere across that narrow strip of water was our army – the BEF (British Expeditionary Force). Some time soon my brother's unit would be joining them. Today I found that hard to believe. Even seeing those boarded-up houses hadn't made the War any more real to me. It seems so very far away – almost as if it's not really happening at all.

Sunday 10 September

I was in the bath this evening when the alarm bell rang. It was our first air-raid warning.

I leaped out of the bath, pulled on my clothes and hared downstairs. I was terrified – my legs jelly on the stairs, gas mask strapped across my chest, tin hat in my shaking hand. After the Roll had been taken we huddled together in the mess, listening – for what? The drone of an enemy plane flying overhead? A bomb dropping on top of us? We clung on to each other – teeth chattering in chorus.

"Are you frightened?" Bunty whispered to me.

"'Course I am," I said. "Aren't you?"

"Terrified," she said.

It wasn't long before the all-clear went – false alarm. A big sigh went up round the room.

My teeth were still chattering as we went back upstairs. "Are you still scared?" Bunty asked me.

"I'm cold. I was having a bath when the alarm went."

"Honest?"

"Honest!"

Monday 11 September

One of the first things a VAD learns is where the bedpans are kept. This morning, when the cry went up, I dashed as usual into the annexe to fetch one. As fast as I could I pulled screens round my patient's bed. Next I had to slide the thing under the patient's body. This is *never* an easy job – you have the pan in one hand, and have to help hoist the patient up with the other. Afterwards, I carefully remove the pan, cover it with a cloth and slowly walk across the ward to the annexe where the pans are cleaned. Only this morning I forgot to cover it! Sister nearly had a fit when she saw me carry the full pan back across the ward.

After that I felt awfully jumpy, and my fingers were all thumbs. This afternoon I dropped the sterile Cheatle forceps on the floor with a clang. Then it took me ages before I got the water the right temperature for a patient's bath. At that, even nice Nurse Winter lost patience with me. By the time I went off duty I was dog-tired and practically in tears. Out of the corner of my eye I could see Sister smiling – actually smiling! – at Nurse Mason.

I looked back as the ward doors closed behind me.

Nurse Mason was wheeling the dressing trolley over to Corporal Smart's bed. I saw her lift the forceps out of the jar. I turned away then. I didn't want to see any more. I just knew that Nurse Mason wouldn't drop them.

Not like me.

Tuesday 12 September

I gave myself a bit of a talking-to last night. I have resolved that:

I must not let Sister Rook upset me. She's right to criticize me when I make mistakes.

I must never forget that I'm here to look after the patients. That's more important than anything else.

The talking-to seemed to have worked. I didn't make a single mistake all morning!

My first shift ended at two today and off I went to have my vaccinations. We all have to have these to protect us from serious diseases like smallpox and typhoid. I was back on duty at five, but my arm felt hot and heavy and by six o'clock I was feeling very wobbly. Sister glanced at me, laid a cool dry hand on my forehead, and jabbed a thermometer in my mouth. 100 degrees! She told me to go to bed and to stay there until my temperature had come down. Her voice was unusually gentle. Most surprising.

My temperature was up again this evening. I'm sure that tossing and turning on those awful army biscuits didn't help.

Something else surprising – Nurse Mason must have brought me a mug of tea. I found it – cold – when I woke up.

Wednesday 13 September

My arm's still rather stiff, but my temperature's down so it was back on duty for me.

Our youngest QA – Nurse Green – was in such a flap this morning. One of our patients – Private Johnson – was due to be discharged back to his regiment today. Suddenly his temperature shot up. 103!

It was very odd. He'd seemed all right at breakfast. And then I saw the mug of tea on his locker. Of course it was obvious then what Private Johnson had done – he'd stuck the thermometer in the mug of hot tea. It's an old, old trick. I went up to Nurse Green.

"Nurse Green," I said shyly, pointing to the mug. "Do you think that . . . maybe. . .?"

She wouldn't even let me finish. "Don't be ridiculous, Nurse Langley," she snapped.

I caught Molly's eye. Her eyes widened when I pointed out the mug. We grinned at each other, and then I turned back to find Nurse Green glaring at me so I hopped off to my duties.

Sister had popped out, so Nurse Green went to fetch a doctor. It wasn't Major Roberts who came, it was a tall, young doctor I'd not seen before. He strode up to the bed, looking awfully keen. "A real case for me," his face seemed to say. It was such a nice face too, I thought.

Nurse Green explained the problem and the MO nodded seriously. He took Johnson's wrist in his fingers and checked his pulse. Then I watched as he got out his stethoscope to listen to his chest, and then he began to prod and pull Johnson all over the place. He looked very puzzled. He hadn't seen the mug of tea. I wished I could tell him about it, but I was only a VAD and we VADs are *not* supposed to talk to the doctors.

Johnson just lay there, eyes shut, though I saw him wince once or twice.

Then Sister reappeared, and the MO explained his findings. Sister nodded her head. She looked at Johnson.

"Now, Johnson, what's all this?" I heard her ask him briskly.

"Oh, Sister, I come over all bad. Very sudden it was," he

said, eyes still firmly shut. Sister nodded grimly and thrust the thermometer back in Johnson's open mouth. After a minute she took it out and examined it.

"Well, it's back to normal now," she said. "You seem to have made an equally sudden recovery." I saw her reach up to the bedside locker. She picked up the mug.

Sister Rook just looked at Nurse Green. She didn't need to say anything. Nurse Green got out a handkerchief and pretended to blow her nose, but we could all see how red her face had gone behind it. I looked down at my feet.

"Thank you, Lieutenant," Sister Rook said, turning to the MO. The expression on her face was clear enough. Major Roberts would never have made a mistake like that. I felt sorry for the MO then.

Sister Rook pursed up her lips in that way of hers and looked at her patient firmly. Johnson just rolled his eyes and shrugged his shoulders. I suppose he'd thought it worth a try.

Nurse Green was on the mat for that, and Sister looked more and more sour as the day went on. It was all "sweep up that fluff!" (there wasn't any) and "why's that patient's sheet not straight?" (it was!). I was very relieved when it was five o'clock and I went off duty.

Bunty and Marjorie were also finishing at five today and they asked me to come into town with them, but my arm was still sore and all I wanted to do was crawl upstairs to bed. It's all I ever want to do when I go off duty. My arms have sprouted muscles I never knew I had from heaving that bumper about. My feet and back ache constantly from standing all day long. As for my hands – already they're rough and red from all the washing and cleaning. Sister's hands are as soft as a baby's. I don't know what her secret is but Bunty reckons it's because she spends more time in the duty room with our MO than on the ward. She says everyone knows that Sister Rook has a soft spot for Major Roberts. That did make us laugh. I even saw Nurse Mason's lips twitch. If you knew Major Roberts you'd understand why.

I *still* don't know Nurse Mason's first name, and wonder if she'll ever tell me it. She's awfully proper. We're all rather in awe of her – even Bunty.

Thursday 14 September

Letter from Anne today! When it was time for my break I settled down to read it.

"Dear Kitten, It's so awful that you're down there and I'm up here in Leeds. I do *not* like it here. The hospital's outside the town, it rains all the time and I don't know a soul. Food's awful. Sister's a little tyrant. We spend most of our time cleaning!

"Are the rest of the St Jude's gang there? Remember me to them.

"Wish I was there – or you here. I miss you so much.

"Are you keeping up your diary? I am! Please write soon. I want lots of gossip. Better stop now – or I'll be late for work and Sister will eat me alive."

I turned the page over. Anne had scribbled a brief PS on the back: "Have you heard from Giles yet? I'll bet he looks dashing in his pilot's uniform."

I *haven't* heard from Giles yet. Giles is sort of my boyfriend. I met him at a village dance earlier this summer and he told me he was joining the RAF. He wants to train as a fighter pilot. Anyway, he asked if he could write to me and would I write back. I felt very flattered – he's awfully handsome – and I liked him too, so I said that I would. I wonder when I'll hear from him. I've been here nearly two weeks now and not a squeak from him. I'm beginning to think he's forgotten me already.

Friday 15 September

I had a bit of a grumble to Molly about Sister today and . . . and . . . well, about *everything*. Like all the silly rules, that clicking of heels, and that to-do about how the patients lay in bed when the Colonel did his inspection. It seemed all wrong to me. "Their comfort should come first," I said to Molly vehemently.

And lastly, I aired my favourite grumble – when when when would I get the chance to do some proper nursing?

"When I can trust you, Nurse Langley," I thought I heard someone say. A moment later I saw Sister sail past us. Was that her voice in my ear, or just a tiny voice inside my head? It's been puzzling me all afternoon, and I just don't know the answer.

Monday 18 September

I got my first-ever letter from Giles today. I was so pleased when I saw it waiting for me – raced off straightaway to read it – but now I just feel miserable.

It was all about the planes he's learning to fly – lots of technical stuff that's too boring to write here. It wasn't what I'd been expecting at all. Then at the end he wrote: "Ripping that you said you'd write to me. Please write back – soon." He sounded a bit lonely – and suddenly I felt sorry for him. But I don't want to feel *sorry* for him – not if he's to be my boyfriend. Oh bother, I don't know what I feel – or what he feels about me! I wish there was someone I could talk to about Giles – someone who really knows him.

I'd been so looking forward to hearing from him. And I know I must write back soon, but now I just don't know what to say to him.

Monday 25 September

Weekly gas drill this morning. For half an hour we had to do the chores with our gas masks and tin hats on. I always want to giggle when I see Sister Rook in hers – today I did, and then my mask misted up and I tripped up over Private Baker's boots. I made a grab for the bedpost and righted myself just in time. Luckily Sister didn't notice, or I'd have been in trouble again.

It's a week now since I had my letter from Giles but I only sat down to answer it today. My first attempt was awfully stilted – all about my work on the wards. It was quite as dull as his. So I tried again. I told myself to forget the awfully unsatisfactory letter I'd got from him and just think about the boy I'd met and how much I'd liked him. That made it much easier and I got on swimmingly. I feel a lot happier now. What does one silly letter matter anyway?

Wednesday 27 September

This evening I saw a bunch of VADs clustered round the notice board in the mess. I couldn't get close enough to see what the fuss was all about, but Molly saw me and called me over.

"We've been asked to a regimental dance," she said excitedly, waving a finger at the board.

I'm thrilled! I've never been to a regimental dance before! Bunty's already planning to go into town first to get her hair done. I don't know how she thinks she'll find the time. Marjorie's going round with a long face. Poor Marjorie. She's just started on night duty and so will miss all the fun.

Friday 29 September

Molly and I are so envious of Nurse Mason! She's won Sister's trust – the first of us three to do so. So now she's being allowed to take the patients' temperature, pulse and respiration – a very responsible job. (Doing the TPRs we call this.) And it's all thanks to Molly's infected hand.

We were in the annexe today, putting away the cleaning things, when I heard Nurse Mason exclaim: "Nurse Smythe – your hand!" She sounded really shocked. Molly looked down at it and tucked it out of sight at once, but Nurse Mason asked if she could have a look. Slowly Molly held out her hand and Nurse Mason took it in hers and turned it over. It was very inflamed and sore-looking. As Nurse Mason was inspecting it, I noticed *her* hands too. I was startled. They look as soft and white as Sister's, yet Nurse Mason spends just as much time cleaning as Molly and me.

"You need to get that treated," she said at last, putting Molly's hand down gently. Then she had a look at Molly's other hand. It, too, was all red and cracked. I clasped my own roughened hands behind my back, feeling rather ashamed of them.

"Make sure you put plenty of cream on that hand," she told Molly firmly. "Germs can get into the cracks. You don't want it to get infected, do you?"

Molly looked awfully sheepish, but before she could say anything Sister's voice cut in.

"Nurse Smythe, Nurse Mason, I'd like a word with you." We all jumped – even Nurse Mason! I wish Sister wouldn't creep up on us like that.

Poor Molly! When Sister Rook saw her hands she gave her such a wigging. Afterwards she shooed her into the treatment room and then she beckoned Nurse Mason over. I thought she was going to get a telling off too – for talking – but Sister Rook was smiling now. I wondered what Sister was saying to her.

Later this morning I found out. Nurse Mason walked up to a patient, a thermometer in her hand. She popped it into his mouth. I thought I'd drop through the floor! Then she put a finger on her patient's pulse to check that that was normal too and looked carefully at him to check his breathing.

Nurse Mason was doing the TPRs! I looked at her face. I thought she'd be thrilled, but she looked just the same as she always does.

As for me, I was still in shock. But I'm not surprised that she's won Sister's trust. Nurse Mason *is* a jolly good VAD.

She's not popular amongst the VADs though. This evening when we left Ward B I heard some VADs giggling about her in the corridor.

"Nurse Mason's nickname's Titch," one of them said.

"Maybe that will bring her down to size," another voice said, giggling.

"Oh, don't be so unkind. She's not that bad," I heard someone burst out suddenly. Me! They looked round, surprised.

"It's Nurse Mason's roommate," I heard one of them whisper as I stalked off.

It's true, I don't dislike Nurse Mason, I just feel I don't know her any better than when we came. She's very reserved. Whenever I try to talk to her all I get is "yes" or "no".

Later I asked Bunty if *she's* got a nickname yet. She went pink, but she won't say.

Sunday 1 October

My first whole day's leave – I spent it at home! I caught the train and Mother met me at the other end. Fell off the train into her arms. I gave her a huge hug – I was so pleased to see her. She held me away from her for a moment.

"Darling, you're so thin!" she said, sounding horrified. I told her I was fine but I ate every morsel at lunch. Seconds too. Roast beef and Yorkshire pud, trifle to follow. Delish! We're not badly fed at the hospital but the food's very dull and I'm always hungry.

The house seemed awfully quiet without Father and Peter. Peter's still training with his unit. And Father?

"He couldn't get any time off," said Mother sadly. She said

he's not allowed to tell her anything about his work for the government – it's top secret. Poor Mother. I think she gets pretty lonely, and now Cook's been talking about joining up. So Mother's wondering whether she should join up too.

We listened to Mr Churchill, one of the government ministers, on the wireless. The news is awful. Poland's finally fallen to the enemy.

We British just stood by and watched while our ally, Poland, was invaded. Now the country's being divided up between Germany and Soviet Russia. I think we should be ashamed that we allowed it to happen.

Afterwards, Mother and I went for a brisk walk. We didn't talk any more about the War. She asked me about my work but I quickly changed the subject. For those few precious hours I wanted to forget all about the War – and the hospital.

I felt sad as we drove away from the house. I knew it might be a long time before I could come home again.

When Mother dropped me off at the station, she handed me a bulky package.

"It's a surprise," she smiled. "Open it when you get back."

As soon as I was alone in my room, I opened Mother's parcel. Cake, biscuits, chocolate, fruit tumbled out on to the bed. I felt a bit tearful as I looked at it lying there. Mother's so good to me. Then Nurse Mason walked in and just stared at it all. It did look awful – all that food strewn over my bed – and suddenly I felt very embarrassed. Timidly I asked her to help herself, and eventually she took one biscuit, but she did so very reluctantly. She looked as if she wanted to say something, but she didn't. My roommate is *such* a puzzle still. But at least she's told me her first name now. It's Jean.

Friday 6 October

There are two good things about all the cleaning we have to do. Firstly, it helps keep our patients free of infection. That makes us very proud. And it's when I go round the beds each day, pulling them out, scrubbing and tidying the lockers, polishing the bedsteads, that I can lean over and talk to my patients. For me this is the best thing about being a VAD.

Underneath all their cheek I've come to realize that our patients are just awfully homesick. For most of them it's their first time ever away from home. I want to help them, and I hope that I do, even if it's just little things like this and not the proper nursing I long to do. And as soon as they're well, they're back to their regiments – and danger. I never let myself forget that.

Saturday 7 October

The big day today – and my busiest yet on Ward B. We're short-staffed, as Molly's off sick with her bad hand, and now Nurse Winter's gone down with flu. I don't know how we got all the work done this morning and, to make matters worse, every time I looked up I saw Sister Rook's eyes clamped on me. As the afternoon drew on I was feeling more and more excited. I glanced at the ward clock. Quarter to five. In just fifteen minutes I'd go off duty – so long as Sister didn't want me to do anything else. I tiptoed past her office into the ward kitchen, to make a cup of tea for one of the patients, hoping she wouldn't notice me. I was just tiptoeing back on to the ward again when she shot out of her room. I was so startled that I nearly dropped the cup.

"Nurse Langley, I'd like you to do something for me," she said, as though she was doing me a huge favour.

"Yes, Sister," I said, wondering what she wanted me to do. Was she beginning to trust me at last?

"I need someone to do Private Morris's pressure points. We don't want him to get any bedsores, do we?"

Ugh! Bedsores are one of Sister's Big Things and now I had to listen to her on the subject again. Out of the corner of one eye I saw the hands of the ward clock reach five. Sister was still talking.

"None of my patients ever gets a bedsore!" she said, giving me one of her beady looks.

"Yes, Sister," I said obediently.

It's a horrible job – and it takes ages. When at last I was allowed off duty it was getting on for six and I was dog-tired. I raced off for a bath. I was yearning for a good long soak, but you can't, not in the shallow bath we're allowed here – five inches deep at most. Anyway, I didn't have time now. I leaned back in the tub, watching the steam fill the cubicle, and then I closed my eyes.

Half an hour later I heard someone bang on the bathroom door. I'd nodded off! Still damp from my bath, I belted back to my room. My clothes were laid out ready on the bed, cap freshly made up, but I was in such a hurry by now that I put my heel through my last good pair of stockings. Proper silk ones too! Bunty came to my aid and we did a hasty repair job – dabbing mascara on the pink bits that showed. We raced up to the bus, greatcoats flapping round our shoulders. The driver tooted his horn. We climbed on board just as the bus was pulling out. I had to do my make-up in the back as the bus lurched off down the drive.

The dance was jolly good fun. There was a real band: it was thumping away as we entered – a bit shyly. We VADs were awfully popular, we soon discovered, as there were at least twice the number of men to girls, but after only a couple of dances my feet were killing me and I had to turn down several partners.

Then a Second Lieutenant came up and asked me to dance. I was about to turn him down too, when he blurted out: "We're going to France." He looked excited – and so heartbreakingly young. I felt I *had* to dance with him then.

"My brother's unit will be out there soon too," I told him, trying to stop my voice from wobbling.

"Jolly good show," he said approvingly, and he held out his hand to swing me in to the dance.

As soon as we'd arrived Bunty had vanished into the hot, smoky room, but when my dance was over she suddenly appeared at my shoulder.

"What are you doing?" I said, annoyed, as she hauled me away from the dance floor.

"Your heels," she hissed. I looked down. Great gaping pink bits! In *both* of them!

"Oh, Bunty," I wailed.

"Never mind. We'll soon fix it," she said, fishing mascara out of her handbag.

She looked over my shoulder. "Wait a jif! That officer's coming back." I pulled a face.

"What's wrong?" she said. "He looks nice." Then she smiled. "Of course. Silly me. It's Giles, isn't it?"

"Maybe," I said, blushing.

"You've heard from him, haven't you?" she said, eyes twinkling.

I nodded, face scarlet now.

"I'll get rid of him," she whispered.

The officer had reached us now. Bunty turned and smiled at him. "Would you be very kind and fetch me a drink?" she said, batting her eyelashes at him. Bunty's eyelashes are so long, I sometimes wonder if they're real. The officer swallowed and I saw a tide of colour flood his face. Bunty winked at me as he disappeared back into the throng crowding the bar. Then she slipped into the crowd behind him.

I giggled. Bunty's a real friend.

At the end of the evening the band played "We'll Meet Again" and then someone began to sing "Auld Lang Syne" and one by one we all joined in. I had a lump in my throat and some of the girls were a bit tearful as they said goodbye. The regiment leaves in a week.

I didn't see Bunty again until we were back on the bus. She fell asleep, head on my shoulder. She had a big smile on her face.

Sunday 8 October

Half day this morning. Slept and slept and slept. Jean told me the girls popped by to see me, but she wouldn't let them wake me. There's a kind streak in Jean Mason.

I think one of the patients quite likes me. Anyway, he blushed when I took him his supper this evening. And that made *me* blush. It's that young Private – Private Morris. It's drummed into us that we mustn't have favourites amongst the patients, and I do try to treat them all the same. So when I went back to take away his dirty plate I was a bit brisker with him. He gave me such a sad look and I just felt mean. So I gave him a big smile when I said goodnight and he smiled back, all pink again. Oh dear, I just don't know how to treat him.

As I walked past the dorm this evening, Molly saw me. She pounced. "I want to hear all about the dance – Bunty won't tell me anything!" she cried.

Spent the rest of the evening in the dorm, gossiping. Molly told me she thinks Bunty's got a new flame – *I* think I know who it is!

Tuesday 10 October

Went on the ward today to find that screens have been placed round Private Morris's bed. Private Morris has been here the longest of all our patients now.

Our MO was an awfully long time in there with him this morning and his face looked very grave when he came out again. Matron was with him. He had a long murmured conversation with her as they stood outside the screens.

I took Private Morris his lunch. It's not hard to see why the doctors are so worried about him. He's awfully thin and frail.

I sat down next to his bed. I'd cut up his food into little pieces and now I tried to persuade him to eat it. It was awful – after only one mouthful he was sick. He looked up at me shamefacedly.

"I'm sorry, miss, really sorry," he said.

He was sorry! I was almost in tears as I mopped up. I wish there was something more I could do for him. I wish he'd get better.

Wednesday 11 October

I had a bit of a shock when I reported for duty this morning. Private Morris's bed was empty. He's been transferred to another hospital.

I know it's the right decision. I know that there he'll get the specialist care he needs, but I did feel upset. I'd not even been able to say goodbye.

Molly's hand is better now, and after work I cycled into town with her and Bunty. I cheered up a bit then. We stopped at a hotel for drinks because Bunty said she was hot and needed a long drink before cycling back.

She went very red as she said it, and she blushed each time the hotel doors swung open. I felt sure that she was expecting someone, even though she pretended she wasn't. Anyway, whoever it was, they didn't show, and she was quite grumpy on the way back. I asked her what was wrong. She said it was nothing. Nothing! I cycled on ahead. I felt very put out. Why wouldn't she tell me what was going on? I thought she was my friend! And on top of everything else now we were going to be late for Roll Call. Afterwards, I stomped up to my room on my own and spent the next hour writing letters. I tore up my letter to Giles. I can't write to him again. I've got to wait to hear from him first. Anyway, I don't know *what* to say to him. I got into bed to write my diary, still feeling all cross and bothered.

Sunday 15 October

Yesterday I got a scribbled note from Peter. I turned over the envelope and looked at the date. It was two weeks old.

"This is it, Sis," he'd written hastily in pencil. "The lads are off – by the time you get this I'll be in France. Tell Mater not to worry, won't you? Better still, be a love and pop over to see her if you can." That was the gist of it – Peter's not one for letter-writing.

I felt sure that Mother was worried. *I* was worried – terribly worried – and it was that which drove me to go to church. It was a long time since I'd been, but today I felt I simply had to go.

As I walked up to the church something felt wrong. Slowly it dawned on me what it was. The church bells weren't ringing. And they won't ring again until the War's over, unless it's to warn us that the country's been invaded.

All the church bells will ring then. Just thinking about that made me feel a whole lot worse.

I don't think I've ever prayed so hard before. I prayed for Peter – and then I prayed for that regiment. They'll be in France too by now. And then I prayed for Giles. I don't know what to think about Giles. I've still not heard from him. Has something awful happened to him? Or is it simply that he doesn't care any more? I know I shouldn't feel cross – especially not in church – but I did. I just don't know whether I should be worrying about him or not.

Jean was in church too. I saw her, two rows in front of me, when I sat down in my pew again. After the sermon, when we stood for the hymn, she stayed in her seat, head bowed, as though she'd forgotten where she was. And as soon as the service was over she rushed straight out. She looked as if she wanted to be on her own, so I didn't try to catch up with her. I found myself wondering if *she* has someone close – a brother maybe – out in France too.

Spent the evening writing to Anne and Peter and then I went to the VADs' mess to listen to the news on the wireless. Bunty was there. She flushed, and I saw her tuck something hastily away in a pad of paper. She looked up at me and smiled, but it wasn't much of a smile.

I sat down next to her.

"What's wrong, Bunty?" I asked straightaway.

She flushed a deeper shade of pink.

"Come on, Bunty, 'fess," I wheedled.

She looked down at her lap. "Sorry, Kitten, I just – I..."

"It's that Lieutenant, isn't it?" I said abruptly. "The Lieutenant we met at the dance. You like him, don't you?"

She nodded. Her hands were clenched tightly in her lap. "Kitten, I meant to tell you, really I did. But ... oh, Kitten, I do like him, but I don't know what *he* thinks... I'd hoped to see him before he left. I did see him once, and he said he'd try and see me again, but he didn't, and now I don't know what he feels... If he feels..." her voice trailed away again.

"Oh Bunty, I'm sure he wanted to see you!" I burst out. "He'd have had a lot to do before going out to France." I sort of mumbled the last words, for Bunty's face was crumpling again. She blinked her eyes very fast and I felt my eyes prick too. I can't bear thinking about them all out in France.

"How's Giles?" Bunty asked suddenly.

"I don't know," I said slowly. "He hasn't answered my last letter. Oh Bunty, I don't know what to think any more."

"Maybe he's just very busy too," said Bunty. "Or maybe he never even got your letter."

I hadn't thought of that. "Maybe," I said.

I got up and turned up the wireless and we pulled our

chairs up close to the set. Jean came in then. I saw her hesitate when she saw us sitting there so cosily together, so I told her to pull up a chair.

That gloomy newsreader was on again. The news is bad. One of our battleships, *The Royal Oak*, was torpedoed and sunk by a German U-boat in Scapa Flow early yesterday morning. About 700 men drowned – the ship's commander amongst them. I hadn't a clue where Scapa Flow was – neither did Bunty – until Jean told us that it's between the Orkney Islands and the north coast of Scotland. Jean really does know the most extraordinary things.

I think we all felt very down after that, so Jean went down to the kitchen and returned with mugs of steaming cocoa. That cheered us all wonderfully – even Bunty perked up a bit.

Monday 23 October

Today Sister ordered me to help Nurse Winter with a dressing – a kaolin poultice for one of our patients who's got a bad chest.

I was thrilled. After nearly two months here, they'd learn that I did know something.

"We're a bit short of kaolin," Nurse Winter told me, scrubbing her hands thoroughly as she talked, "so we'll have to heat up the old poultice again."

I watched as she inserted the poultice – a piece of lint wrapped round kaolin clay – between two pan lids over boiling water. She talked me through everything she was doing – step by step. I listened obediently, but I was longing to tell her that I'd done this myself before, during my Red Cross training.

I stood by the gleaming dressing tray and watched as Nurse Winter placed the warm poultice in position. She'd asked me to test it first on the back of my hand to make sure it wasn't too hot for our patient's skin. Then she looked up at me. I smiled – I knew what she was going to ask. I moved eagerly round to the far side of the bed.

"Nurse Langley, I need your help again."

"Yes," I said happily.

"We're going to wrap this bandage back around the Corporal to hold the poultice in place. It's called a many-tail bandage."

I know that! I nearly burst out then.

"You did that very nicely, Nurse Langley," Nurse Winter said when we'd finished. She sounded very pleased. I told myself to try and be content with that.

Monday 30 October

We're going to throw a party for the officers. A bossy VAD's formed a committee to take charge of the arrangements. Bunty's joined it and tonight she dragged me along to a meeting. I discovered that I'd already been allocated a task – to organize the dance music. "It's because you're so musical," I was told.

"What?" I exclaimed. Musical is one thing I'm not! And then, out of the corner of my eye I could see that Bunty was splitting her sides. She's been pulling their legs. Bunty's such a tease! I don't know if she's heard from her Lieutenant yet, but I think she must have, for she seems much more cheerful now.

The meeting had just ended when Molly stomped in, face nearly brushing the floor.

"I'm spending the next two weeks typing up forms and medical notes in the office," she declared crossly.

I'd hate to do that job. Luckily, I won't be. I can't type.

Wednesday 8 November

I got another letter from Giles today. It was another blow-by-blow account of what he's doing at his training school. It was pretty dull, though some of the flying does sound very exciting – spins and rolls and things like that. He's hoping to become a Spitfire pilot.

I don't know why he thinks I'd be interested in all that technical stuff. I'm much more interested in how he feels about *me* – and again there was nothing at all in his letter about that. Honestly, you'd think the wretched planes mattered more to him.

I told Bunty that I'd had another letter from Giles. She told me she was relieved. I could tell what she'd been thinking – that sometimes pilots are killed in training. I know that, of course. I just try not to think about it.

Spent the rest of the evening knitting "comforts" for the troops. Marjorie and Molly are knitting scarves. Molly's is already as big as she is! My effort's no better. It's supposed to be a balaclava "helmet". We've been told to leave only very small holes for the eyes. My holes seem to get bigger by the day and it's all sort of bobbly. I feel sorry for the soldier who gets it. I don't think he'll find it very comforting.

Thursday 9 November

At supper this evening Molly told me that Jean Mason has got herself transferred – to the Surgical ward. Molly said that she went up to Matron – Matron! – and actually asked for the transfer. I gaped at her. I'd never dare to be as bold as that.

"She thinks she needs the experience," Molly added.

Poor Molly! She loathes her new job. Our MO's handwriting is the worst, she said. And practically everything has to be typed in triplicate.

She says the MOs hardly ever say a word to her – even when Matron isn't around to check up on them. Already she's desperate to return to the wards.

Sunday 12 November

There's a stack of books on the box by Jean's bed. I'd always assumed they were nursing manuals, but this evening I took a closer look at them. I hadn't meant to be nosy, but I just couldn't help it – the cover of the one on top had caught my eye. It wasn't a nursing manual, it was a book on anatomy. Old, too. Well-thumbed. The sort of book a medical student would study – not a VAD. I knew I shouldn't, but I had a quick peep inside. It looked very complicated. Why, I wondered, did Jean need to know all this stuff? And then I remembered what Molly had told me – about Jean asking Matron if she could transfer to the Surgical ward. I'd always thought there was a bit of a mystery about Jean Mason – and now I felt sure I was right.

There was a name on the book's inside cover. Alastair Mason. The ink had faded so I knew that it must have been written a long time ago. Who was Alastair Mason? I wondered. Was he her father? Was he a doctor?

Suddenly I felt disgusted with myself. What did I think I was doing – prying into matters that weren't anything to do with me? Already I'd found out more than I had any right to know.

Jean came in later and settled down on her bed. I watched as she leaned across and picked up one of the books off the box. Suddenly out it came: "Do you want to be a doctor?" Just like that.

Jean just looked at me. "Yes," she said at last, quietly.

"That's marvellous," I said. "I'm sure you'll be a very good one," I prattled on, without thinking what I was saying. Jean was silent. Her face looked even paler than usual. "It's all right for *you*," her eyes seemed to say.

I stopped. I felt bewildered.

"My father was a doctor," she said abruptly. "I wanted to be one too – always did – but then he died and. . ." She stopped suddenly and looked away.

Slowly I began to piece it all together. All the little things that hadn't made any sense. Like why she'd been upset about our pay and why she's always so reluctant to take even a biscuit from me. She can't share back. She's poor. And worst of all, there wasn't the money to pay for her training.

I felt so sorry for her. I leaned across and touched her hand. Jean smiled tiredly at me. "It's all right," she said.

It wasn't.

Not everyone is as lucky as me. I can't imagine what it must be like not to be able to do something you really want – just because there's no money. Poor Jean. Sometimes life can be so unfair.

I smiled back at her. I'm going to make a real effort to be a friend to Jean – if she'll let me.

Monday 13 November

Molly reported back to Ward B today.

"Missed this, did you?" I murmured to her while we were doing the bumpering this morning.

"Anything's better than working in the office," she said vehemently, forgetting that we were in the middle of the ward. "Oops," she said, clapping a hand to her mouth and looking around nervously in case Sister had heard. The patients giggled.

After we'd finished bumpering, Nurse Winter talked me though a dressing she was doing. On a medical ward they're usually for chest ailments – no nasty wounds to clean. She told me about the first time she saw a dressing being changed on a surgical ward. "I nearly fainted clean away," she laughed. When she says things like that, I'm so relieved that I don't work on a surgical ward.

Sunday 19 November

Arrangements for our party are going swimmingly. *All* the officers from miles around are coming – so the rumour goes. I hope it's wrong. We've booked the upstairs room at The George. It's a large room, but even there we'd never fit them all in.

Monday 20 November

At breakfast today we learned that three soldiers from the British Expeditionary Force arrived on the ward last night. I was in a huge panic as I pushed open the ward doors. What if one of them was Peter? How would I cope? Visions of horrible illnesses kept flashing through my mind. I told myself I was just being silly. But what awful things *do* our soldiers pick up, squelching about in the French mud?

The men seemed quite cheerful when I took round

their milk puddings later on. (And – huge relief! – Peter wasn't one of them.) They told me that they're jolly relieved to be back in Blighty, and to be cared for in a proper hospital. All three of them have bad tummy upsets. I'm not surprised that tummy bugs are rife amongst the men out in France. It can't be easy feeding an army in the field. Our cooks find it hard enough in the hospital kitchen!

Like Peter, these lads are serving in the Infantry but none of them are from his unit. They've quite put our other patients' noses out of joint. We stare at them in awe. They're our first casualties from the Front in France and I think they're enjoying all the fuss. Of course, none of them has seen any action yet.

Tuesday 21 November

Private Abbott, one of our new patients, was awfully sick this morning. His pale face looked up at me as I mopped up around him. "I'm sorry, miss," he said. I smiled brightly at him. I'd only just finished when I noticed that his face was looking a bit green again. Round went the screens, off came the sheets and this time I had to give him a proper wash.

As I did this I noticed that he seemed awfully hot. I went to fetch Sister.

"I think Private Abbott's feverish," I told her. She came over to the bed and took out her thermometer. She started to shake it but suddenly she stopped and handed it to me.

"*You* do it, Nurse Langley," she said. I popped the thermometer into the Private's mouth. I was right – he did have a temperature. 100 degrees. I pulled the blanket down to the bottom of the bed to help cool him. When I looked up I saw that Sister was regarding me thoughtfully.

Our poor Private was still unwell this afternoon. He couldn't keep anything down. I'd just finished mopping up again when Sister's head popped round my shoulder.

"Oh, Nurse, could you do the patients' TPRs for me?"

I looked up at her, cloth in hand. I felt dizzy. I was being asked to do the TPRs. Proper nursing at last. And this was only the beginning. . .

Sister's voice broke into my dream. "The TPRs, please, Nurse Langley!" she said, her old irritable self again.

I didn't hesitate any longer. I was terrified she'd change her mind. I went round that ward, thermometer in hand, feeling so proud. After nearly three months here I actually think Sister's beginning to trust me.

Saturday 25 November

I'm writing this tucked under the bedcovers. It's icy in our room. Anne writes that it's unutterably freezing up in Leeds.

It was the VADs' party tonight. Terrific success, so the officers said. And we had gone to a lot of trouble – decorated the room with streamers and danced to music by Henry Hall and Glen Miller.

Jean Mason came too! I'd bullied her into it – and I'm really glad I did. She looked so happy, a huge beam on her face as she was swung round the dance floor. She looked pretty, too – a bit of colour in her clever face.

After we'd got back, Molly went to fetch cocoa and we chewed over the evening together – all of us, even Jean. We squeezed up together on the beds.

"Why are we whispering?" Bunty said suddenly, quite loudly. "We're not keeping anyone awake."

We were in our tiny room.

Suddenly there was a creak outside the door.

"Madam on patrol," Bunty murmured in a loud whisper. We all shut up at once, and then I heard someone giggle as though she couldn't help herself. It was Jean!

"Who were you dancing with?" Bunty said boldly to Jean, when the creaking had stopped. "He looked nice."

I heard another giggle. It was Jean again.

"Which one do you mean?" she managed to get out through her giggles.

I began to giggle too – helplessly.

"You're hopeless, you two," said Bunty. I couldn't see her face in the dark, but I could sense that she was smiling.

It was nice. I wouldn't say that Jean's absolutely one of the gang now, but I do like her and I can tell that the others are warming to her, too.

It was very late when the girls crept back to the dorm. Jean was already fast asleep on top of her bed. I pulled the blankets up over her. As for me, it's a jolly good thing I don't have to get up at six. From tomorrow I'm on nights. No more Sister Rook. Bliss!

Monday 27 November

Night duty on Ward B is hard work because there's just one Sister and two VADs on duty – Molly and me. Between us we have to do everything.

We reported for duty, sharp at eight. The day staff had

already put up the blackout boards and only a thin light filtered into the ward from Sister's office.

When I arrived she was still closeted with Sister Rook. After Sister Rook had finished handing over, the Night Sister – that's Sister Adams – called us in. I saw a dark head bent over the desk next to her. As we entered, a chair swivelled round and a man looked up and smiled, stretching out long legs. It was the duty MO. His face looked oddly familiar.

And then I remembered. Of course! Private Johnson and the thermometer! I went pink, but I think the MO had forgotten, because he just smiled at me.

Sister Adams has three wards to look after. "So you'll be on your toes," she told us, nodding at Molly and myself. Our most important job, she said, was to keep a watchful eye on the patients. "After you've done the TPRs, don't disturb them again." If we had a problem, she said, we were to go straight to her. "If you can't find *me*, speak to Lieutenant Venables."

I blushed again, thinking about that thermometer, and looked down at my feet.

Sister Adams went round the ward with us, handing out the medicines, while we did the TPRs. Private Abbott smiled sleepily at me as I popped a thermometer into his mouth. He's much better, and I think he'll be going back to France soon, poor boy.

Then Sister was off to the next ward and we were on our own.

We had a whole pile of dressings to make up. In the next hour I think I must have made enough cotton-wool swabs and gauze dressings to supply a regiment. My fingers grew heavy as one by one I packed the dressings into a dressing drum.

At midnight Sister popped into the ward again and we were allowed a short break. I had a bite to eat in the kitchen. Bliss to sit down and rest my aching feet. Then I got up and toured the ward again.

The hours from two to four were the worst of all. I could feel sleepiness creep up my arms and legs. Up and down I walked, up and down, back and forth, willing myself to stay awake. The patients were all fast asleep. How I wished it was me asleep in bed!

At four one of our patients woke up and asked for a cup of tea. After I'd checked his temperature, I took one over to him. He smiled at me as he drank it.

"Missed this in France," he said, smacking his lips.

Molly got us a mug each and I took one into Lieutenant Venables and Sister in the office. It was truly horrible – bright orange – but by then I think we'd have drunk anything.

At half past seven the day staff came on duty. Was I pleased to see them!

"How do you like working on nights?" Molly asked me as we walked slowly down the corridor and up the stairs.

"Ask me when I've woken up," I told her.

Then I did what I'd been longing to do – fell into bed and slept.

Friday 1 December

It was well into the afternoon when I woke today. I begged some food from the nice VAD cook in the kitchen, and then I wrapped up well and went outside. But as soon as I pushed open the door, an icy wind hurled itself at me, so I quickly went back inside again. Polished the buttons on my greatcoat and then I brushed my shoes ready for Parade on Sunday. At five Jean came in and curled up on her bed with a book. It was one of her medical books, I saw. She looked very studious – head down, bedclothes heaped round her shoulders. I didn't want to disturb her so I crept out again and went down to the games room. Played ping-pong for hours. I was wearing my greatcoat, but I still won all the games!

This evening I heard that the Russian army has bombed Helsinki, the capital of Finland. I don't feel at all like playing ping-pong now and yet I know we must do our best to carry on as normal. It's one way we can stand up to the enemy.

I feel so sorry for the Finns. I can't imagine how we'd feel if London was bombed. The news has come as a shock to all of us here.

Sunday 3 December

This morning, after only three hours' sleep, I had to get up and go on Parade. A Very Important Person was paying us a visit. Before I went down I got out my measuring tape and made sure that Jean's dress was the regulation 12 inches from the ground and her apron 2 inches from the hem of her skirt. Then she did the same for me. I was very sleepy still, and couldn't help grumbling as I got dressed.

We stood outside the hospital, all neatly lined up in rows, in our nurses' uniforms. A beastly wind whipped up, and even the trees were shivering as it swept through them – and us. The Commandant marched up to inspect us, accompanied by the Very Important Person.

They were both wearing greatcoats, hats on too. It's all right for *them*, I found myself thinking resentfully. By the time they'd passed by me, the smile had practically frozen on my face and my hands were as blue as my dress.

Afterwards, there was a big race for the electric fire in the VADs' mess. Me, I leaped up the stairs as fast as I could, flung off my uniform and crawled back under the bedclothes. I was still fast asleep when Jean woke me again at lunchtime.

Tuesday 5 December

Lieutenant Venables was on duty again last night. He's not like the other doctors I've worked with here. He's friendly and he always smiles at me and Molly, though he's careful not to talk to us when Sister's around. He confided to me that he's never forgotten Private Johnson and the thermometer. It was his first day at the hospital, he said. It was a most valuable lesson. I bet he got well and truly teased for it.

Anyway, I was just thinking how nice he was when Molly whispered, "What do you think of Lieutenant Venables?"

We were having an early morning cup of tea.

"He seems nice," I said.

He looks a bit like Giles, I found myself thinking suddenly. Or does he? I've been finding it harder and harder to remember what Giles looks like.

Suddenly I remembered – I hadn't answered Giles's last letter! When I went off duty I took it out of the cardboard box where I keep all my letters and looked at the date – 1 November! I felt dreadfully guilty so I sat down and wrote to him straightaway. I told him that I'd been awfully busy, but then so, I'm sure, has he. I hope he'll forgive me. I hope it won't stop him writing to me again.

Thursday 7 December

I fell asleep on duty yesterday. This is an awful crime!

I'd taken a cup of tea over to one of our patients and he'd asked me to stop and chat to him. This is one of the few times that you're allowed to sit down on duty. I sat down gratefully, remembering just in time to pull up the sides of my starched apron so that it wouldn't get creased. Actually, the Corporal didn't want to chat, he just wanted someone to listen. What's more, he had plenty to say, and I felt myself growing more and more sleepy listening to his soft voice.

Suddenly I felt a hand shake my shoulder and I practically jumped out of my chair in terror! In the bed next to me my patient was snoring peacefully.

I was in luck. It wasn't Sister, it was Molly.

"Kitty, your cap!" Molly whispered. My relieved sigh turned to a groan as I put my hand to my head.

If rule number one is: Thou must not fall asleep on duty, rule number two is: Never, ever lean back in a chair or thou wilt crease thy cap. Molly shielded me as best she could – eyes darting round the ward in case Sister appeared – while I tried to repair the damage. If Sister *did* notice, she didn't say anything.

As for me, I've found that I like working on nights. It is awfully tiring, but I relish the extra responsibility. I tiptoe round the ward, glancing at our patients, tweaking a blanket back on to a bed here, fetching a cup of tea there, listening – always listening – to make sure that everyone is settled and sleeping. For a time I can even pretend that I'm a proper nurse. . .

Monday 11 December

The town's been battered by frightful storms. I cannot think what it must be like to be on board ship out on the swelling grey sea. I feel sick just looking at it.

All leave's been cancelled so I won't be able to go home. It'll be my first Christmas ever away from home. Felt awfully choked, and then I reminded myself how much worse it is for our patients.

Monday 18 December

I feel really happy today. Mother's written and told me that they're going to drive down and take me out for lunch on Boxing Day. I feel so touched – they'll probably use up every last drop of their petrol ration. Bunty's told me that she's got her ward – Officers' – making streamers for Christmas.

"I doubt Sister Rook will let anyone put streamers

up on our ward," I said to her. We were curled up on my bed.

"Get that dishy doctor to ask her."

"Who do you mean?" I asked. I wasn't really listening. I was watching how my breath hung in the air – it was freezing in our room. I burrowed deeper under the blankets.

"Kitten, I despair of you, really I do," Bunty said, grinning and pulling the blankets back off me. "Lieutenant what's-his-name."

"Venables," Marjorie said promptly.

"See, Marjorie knows, and she's not even working on your ward. Don't tell me you haven't noticed?"

I just smiled sweetly at her and pulled the blankets totally over my head.

Monday 25 December

Woke in time for Christmas lunch, which we had in the VADs' mess. The long tables looked so pretty – holly and candles on the starched white tablecloths. Our cooks had done us proud; just like at home we had turkey and all the trimmings; there was even Christmas pudding – about a

80

mouthful each. One of the VADs who'd been on leave had brought back crackers. Someone tried to put a paper hat on, but she couldn't get it on over her white cap.

Soon the whole table was shrieking with laughter – hats toppling off caps. Then Madam came in and we whipped them off. Her face creased into a big smile as her gaze swept the tables. I think she was pleased to see our happy faces.

We'd barely finished our meal when all the lights went out. Pandemonium! A tree had toppled over in the high winds, bringing down one of the lines near the hospital, and all the power failed. Later we found out that in the midst of it all, an emergency appendix was brought in and they had to operate by hurricane lamp. The poor VAD on duty had to sterilize all the surgical instruments on top of primus stoves as the sterilizers weren't working. At least – being Christmas – it was the only operation they had to do today.

After lunch, I popped into the ward to wish our patients a happy Christmas. I gasped when I pushed open the door. It was festooned with greenery and many of the patients had cards by their beds. One of them whipped out a sprig of mistletoe from behind his pillow and asked for a kiss! So embarrassing! Another gave me a bar of chocolate. I felt really pleased and handed round the cards I'd got for everyone.

Lieutenant Venables was there, too. He waved at me

across the ward and then he came over to wish me a happy Christmas. Then suddenly I remembered what Bunty had said about him and I felt this huge blush flood my face. I don't know what he must have thought of me.

Tuesday 26 December

Writing this hurriedly before going on duty. Heavenly day. When Mother met me at the hospital she told me there was a surprise waiting for me in the car. She had a big smile on her face but I couldn't guess – so I rushed out ahead of her.

Inside the car, two faces beamed out at me. Father – and Peter!

It was absolutely my bestest Christmas present ever!

Monday 1 January 1940

I'm writing this at home. I finished my first bout of night duty a few days ago and so I have four nights and days off – bliss!

Father's away, and Peter of course has gone back to France. We don't often talk about the War, but on Boxing Day I'd asked him to tell me what it was like across the Channel. Not a lot's been happening, he told me. No one's fired a shot yet, except in training. His unit's been busy digging anti-tank ditches and spreading wire and he's also been working on the roads. He looked awfully tired, but fit. He pretended to be shocked when he saw me and said that my arm muscles were bigger than his! "You'll never get a husband now, Sis," he joked. He told me that he knew what we VADs are nicknamed and when the parents weren't listening he whispered it in my ear. (Unrepeatable!)

Giles has been on leave, too, and yesterday evening he came over and we went to the flicks together. I'd felt very pleased when he rang to ask me out – I hadn't expected him to – he hadn't answered my last letter. He looked awfully handsome in his powder-blue pilot's uniform and flying cap. I was glad I'd dolled up – I spent ages in the bathroom, as it was a special occasion! And I was wearing the lipstick Peter gave me for Christmas. Bright red too!

In the cinema, as soon as the lights had dimmed, Giles took my hand. I thought I'd feel pleased, but I didn't – somehow it felt all wrong. When the lights came on again he snatched away his hand, as if he felt awkward too.

But later he tried a kiss, in the car as he dropped me off. That felt wrong, too. We sat in the car for a minute in silence.

"I nearly didn't call you," he said at last, giving me a sidelong look. "I wasn't sure you wanted to see me." He hesitated. "When you didn't answer my letter for so long I wondered – I wondered if you'd met anyone else. I didn't write again because I didn't know what to say." He turned quickly away and looked out of the window, as if he thought he'd see my answer in my face and was secretly dreading it.

"I haven't—" I began. I was about to explain how I felt, when I saw him smile; he looked hugely relieved. I just couldn't tell him the truth then – that I didn't feel for him the way he felt for me. He promised that he'd write and he gave me a quick peck on the cheek. He was rather subdued, and I felt a bit tearful, and I'm sure he thought it was because of him, but it wasn't, or rather it was, but not in the way he thought. Giles is nice, and he's very good-looking, but all evening I'd felt as if he was a stranger.

At breakfast this morning *I* was very subdued. Mother kept glancing at me across the table, but she didn't say anything. Afterwards, when I went upstairs to pack, she came into my bedroom – to help me, she said – but I knew she wanted to find out how my evening with Giles had gone.

"Well?" she said at last, when I still didn't say anything. She looked worried. Now is not a good time to fall in love – especially with a pilot.

Suddenly I felt a big gush of misery. I flopped down on the bed.

"Oh, Mother, I don't know," I wailed. I told her that I wasn't sure I'd see him again. That I wasn't even sure I wanted to. And . . . and. . . All at once I felt my lips tremble.

"Oh, my poor Kitten," Mother said, hugging me, as if she knew all too well what I was feeling. "It's not easy, is it? Being young." I shook my head, trying to smile, but I felt all choked up inside.

Tuesday 2 January

There was a letter from Anne waiting for me when I got back. It's been ages since I heard from her. I tore it open eagerly. There was a lot about the awful weather up in Leeds, and that she was trying to get transferred south. That wasn't all.

"Giles sounds such a stick," she said. (I'd told her about my unsatisfactory letters from him.) "Poor Kitten! Don't worry about it. You can do a lot better."

At that I just laid my head down on my arms and cried.

Wednesday 3 January

It's all round the hospital how plucky the Finns have been. The story goes that they've made a new sort of weapon to hurl at the Russian army's tanks. It's a grenade, nicknamed a "Molotov cocktail" after Molotov, one of the Russian ministers. Anyway, the Russians were very surprised to find that the Finns didn't surrender straightaway, as next to Soviet Russia, Finland's just a small country. Three cheers for the Finns I say! I hope *we* show as much courage when it's our turn to face the enemy.

Here in the hospital *our* worst enemy is the snow. Last night it fell thickly again. When I took down the blackout boards on the ward this morning, I gasped. The world had turned white. Later in the day, I was woken by tyres skidding outside the hospital and a barrage of hooting. Half asleep still, I went to the window and looked out. An ambulance was desperately trying to get through the snow. In front of it, a lorry was stuck fast. There were soldiers swarming all around it, trying to get it moving again. One of them even put his shoulder to it and tried to push it up the drive!

A minute later the ambulance doors opened and a stretcher was carefully passed down. The stretcher bearers walked slowly through the snow to the hospital, eyes fixed on the ground in case they slipped.

Sister Adams was looking rather flushed last night and I heard her sneezing when I went past the office. There's been an outbreak of influenza in the hospital. I do hope she's not going to be its next victim.

Wednesday 10 January

Absolute pandemonium!

The hospital's overflowing with cases of influenza – both patients and staff. In our ward first it was Sister Adams, and now poor Molly's sick. The patients have had to be shifted in and out of wards, and forms have to be filled in each time someone's moved. I'm amazed we've not lost anyone yet.

Yesterday we ran out of beds and the stretcher bearers had to dump the stretchers on the floor between the beds, their occupants still in them. When I came on duty last night, Sister took me on one side. She told me that she'd asked for extra help, but that there isn't any.

All the other hospitals in the area have been hit hard by flu, too.

Between the two of us we have to do everything: settle the patients down for the night – including all the extra ones, who're still lying on the floor – take round the medicines, give injections and do the TPRs. A lot of this will be down to me now as Sister will be flitting through the other wards in her charge. She told me to call Matron or the duty MO if there were any emergencies. I felt really scared but I knew I just had to knuckle down. I've always wanted responsibility. Well, now I've got it.

Several of our patients have bronchitis and we're afraid that we might have a case of pneumonia on our hands, too. Even our marvellous new drug – M&B693 – cannot always cure pneumonia and the illness requires very careful nursing. And Sister Adams is still a bit weak after her illness. Just how we'd cope I cannot imagine.

Friday 12 January

Thomson developed pneumonia on Wednesday night and we had to move him into a side room. That first night I spent most of my time running in and out of it – and once we had to redo his kaolin poultice, which he'd been given to soothe the pain in his chest. It gets worse when he coughs, which is often. Then every four hours Sister popped by to give him his medicine.

We were so busy! Last night, though, there was another VAD to help us. My word, weren't we pleased to see her! If I hadn't been so busy, I'd have smiled at her nervous, eager expression as she hovered at the ward door – so like me, the day I began. I find it hard to believe that was only a few short months ago. Sister asked her to "special nurse" Thomson, and so she sat down obediently by his bed and glued her eyes to him.

"Any change in his condition must be reported to me at once," Sister told us firmly. "If you can't find me, tell the MO."

Our new VAD nodded, eyes still stuck on Thomson. She looked terrified, so after a while, I went up to check that everything was all right. At about one o'clock she looked as though she was struggling to stay awake so I told her to make us all a mug of Ovaltine. She looked very relieved as she scampered off to the ward kitchen. I sat down in her place. Poor Thomson's breathing still sounded awfully heavy so I propped him up a little on his pillow and gently rubbed his back. Sister had been called to another sick patient and I prayed I wouldn't need to call our MO. We're woefully short of doctors now, as so many of them are down with flu, and poor Lieutenant Venables is rushed off his feet.

At four o'clock I did have to run for the doctor. Our new VAD had told me that Thomson was awake but behaving very strangely. "I think he's hallucinating," she told me anxiously.

Lieutenant Venables looked at Thomson attentively. His breathing sounded better but he was gibbering away. Then he turned and looked full at the doctor.

"Good morning, Sister," he said, smiling brightly.

A broad smile spread over the doctor's face. He told us not to worry that Thomson was talking nonsense. "It's just one of the side effects of the medicine," he whispered. But just to make sure, he gave Thomson a quick check-up before he was called away again, and then I reported to Sister when she came back on to the ward.

I felt a bit of an idiot, but very relieved. Lieutenant Venables is so dependable. It's such a relief to know that I can call on him.

Thomson pulled through the night and I collapsed into bed and slept and slept and slept. Jean looks exhausted and even paler than usual. I do hope she's not going to be ill next.

Sunday 14 January

No more new cases of flu today, but we're still very overstretched on the ward. I'm sure that's why I left an unwashed glass on the ward table when I came off duty early this morning.

I'd been in bed for about an hour when I was woken by a knock on the door. One of our new VADs told me that Sister wanted to see me. Her face looked very apprehensive. What could Sister Rook want? I wondered tiredly, sitting up and rubbing my eyes. I got dressed in my uniform, and made my way sleepily back down to the ward.

It wasn't Sister Rook who was glaring at me in the office – it was a Sister I didn't know, Sister Richardson. Sister Rook's ill, she said shortly, when I asked.

I couldn't think why I'd been summoned, but I was soon to find out. Sister marched me straight into the centre of the ward and pointed at the table.

"What is the meaning of this?" she said.

Every bed in that ward was full, but you could have heard a pin drop. The VAD who'd come to get me stopped what she was doing. Her face was crimson. I didn't know what Sister was talking about. I looked blankly at the table.

"Well, Nurse!" said Sister.

Well, *what*? I thought.

She gave a deep sigh, as if she thought I was really stupid. Then she leaned over the table, picked up a glass and handed it to me.

"This," she said, "was found – unwashed, Nurse – when I came on duty this morning. I was told that you left it there."

I'd forgotten all about that glass.

I began to feel angry. Three months earlier I'd probably have blushed and apologized, but not now. I'd been working nights with very little help for weeks on end, and now I was being hauled in – for this! I knew that glass had been left there to humiliate me – in front of all the patients too. I felt so upset. I wanted to walk out of the ward, down the passage and out of the hospital and never come back. Instead, I took a deep breath, picked up the glass, marched into the annexe, washed it, put it away in its proper place and marched out of the ward again, head held high.

Sister just stood there, watching me. I'd thought Sister Rook was tough. She is, but she isn't petty like Sister Richardson.

Who, I wondered, had told her that I'd left that glass there? Someone who was scared of Sister, a little voice whispered inside my head. Someone like that new little VAD who'd been sent to get me. I knew who I felt sorry for then.

Back in bed again I pulled the bedclothes up over my head. I've been made to look a fool in front of all my patients. I don't know how I'm going to face them again.

When Jean came in I poured out the whole story.

"I don't think you'll have a problem with the patients," she said. Oh, I pray she's right.

Monday 15 January

Jean *was* right. When I went on duty last night the patients smiled at me and for once they all did exactly as I asked. In a quiet moment, one of them beckoned me over. "This is for you, Nurse," he whispered, holding out some chocolate. I think it was the first time any of my patients had called me nurse. I nearly did burst into tears then.

Monday 5 February

I was transferred to the Surgical ward today. Jean and I are both pleased about this – we're working together again.

My first proper job was to "special" a patient, who'd had his appendix removed and was recovering in a side room.

"His temperature's a little high," Sister told me. "I'd like you to do the 'obs' every half an hour."

"Yes, Sister," I said, and leaned over my patient to pop a thermometer into his mouth. And his temperature *was* high. Sister had told me that he'd had his operation two days ago.

The next "obs" I had to do was check my patient's pulse and breathing.

Later, the surgeon popped round to see our patient. Sister unrolled the bandage from his tummy and the surgeon bent over the wound to examine it. It wasn't red, hot or swollen – the tell-tale signs of infection. He checked his patient's pulse. It wasn't too fast. No clots in the lung to worry about either, then.

After the surgeon had gone, the door to the side room opened again. It was Jean with a cup of tea for me. Was I pleased to see it – and her.

"I'm not sure you deserve this," she said, pretending to be annoyed. "I wish I'd been able to spend my morning sitting in a chair."

By lunch time my patient's temperature had started to come down and he smiled at me for the first time. Sister came in and told me to reduce his obs to two-hourly. She looked awfully pleased. That moment when a patient starts to get better – there's nothing like it.

In the afternoon I had to keep an eye on a patient who'd been sick. After they come round from surgery patients are often sick. Luckily I was to hand when I saw him struggle to sit up. He looked at me. I knew that look.

"Oh, miss, I feel awfully dizzy," he murmured. I thrust a bowl under his mouth just in time, and then I propped him up and Sister told me to give him a little warm water and bicarbonate of soda to sip. Even with that the poor boy was sick again. Three times I had to clean up after him.

Tuesday 13 February

It was tea time and I was doing the TPRs. I was the only nurse on the ward, but I'd done the TPRs many times before. There was nothing to worry about.

Holding the thermometer tightly between thumb and forefinger, I shook it firmly downwards.

I looked down in dismay. My hand was empty. The thermometer had smashed on my starched apron. I needed a new one – fast.

I scrabbled helplessly on the floor, trying to find the broken bits. Without them I'd never be allowed a new one. I couldn't find any of it! The bits had simply vanished – rolled under a floorboard or behind a piece of furniture. Empty-handed I raced up to the Quartermaster's office. I told him what had happened. For a full five minutes I pleaded with him.

"Rules is rules," he said. But at last, grudgingly, he agreed to replace it. He was *not* pleased. Even then I wasn't allowed to take the new thermometer away with me. First I had to fill in a form, saying what had happened to the wretched thing, and then I had to get it signed by an MO.

It's another of those mysterious army rules that I find so baffling.

Only then did it dawn on me that the patients were probably still on their own. I tore back to the ward. Ahead of me someone was advancing slowly towards the ward. Matron! I looked at her back in horror. What would she think when she discovered that the patients were on their own? I'll really be on the mat for this, I thought despairingly. I watched as she opened the doors. Legs like jelly, I crept in behind her.

My luck was in. The patients weren't on their own! Jean was back! Later, she explained. "I saw you vanish down the corridor so I came back straightaway."

I was so relieved that I could have hugged her.

"You were lucky," said Bunty, when I told the girls later. "Let me tell you about the time that happened to me."

"Did it really happen to you, too?" Molly asked, wide-eyed.

"Oh yes," she said airily.

"Were you in awful trouble?" Molly asked.

"Oh no. The patients covered for me! They said I was in the annexe – by the time Matron had searched every corner of it, I'd nipped back into the ward. Matron didn't know quite what to think. It was a pretty close shave though."

"Bunty!" gasped Molly.

I gave Bunty a searching look. "Really?" I said.

Bunty's lips were twitching. Suddenly a big laugh burst out of her. "Oh, you are such sillies! Of course not," she said.

Wednesday 14 February

Just before I went off duty this evening, the stretcher bearers rushed into the ward. There'd been a motorcycle accident. Its rider skidded on the wet road and crashed into a tree. As there are no streetlights now because of the blackout it's very hard to see anything at all outside at night – and it's especially a problem now the days are so short. Jean says that there have been several motorcycle crashes since she started work on the Surgical ward. It reminded me that we're at war. It probably sounds peculiar, but sometimes I forget that. In this hospital, with no war casualties to deal with yet, we're cocooned from the worst of it.

I'm in such a spot. I've had a letter from Giles and I don't know what to say to him.

Thursday 15 February

This morning the doors had barely shut behind the Colonel and his party, when the stretcher bearers rushed in again. Another motorcycle accident. Another broken leg.

While we were waiting for our patient to return to the ward – leg swathed in Plaster of Paris – we prepared a special bed for him. It would be twelve or more hours before the plaster set, and we needed to keep the leg absolutely straight, so I held up the mattress while one of our QAs – Nurse Jackson – put boards over the bed's metal frame. Then we lifted the foot of the bed and put blocks underneath to raise it. This would help our patient's blood flow the right way – towards his heart and head. That's important when the patient can't move around in bed.

The plaster was still damp when our patient was put to bed, so we put a mackintosh sheet under him to keep him dry. Then Nurse Jackson put a special cradle over his leg to keep the bedclothes off it while I was sent off to fill up some hot-water bottles.

When I returned with the filled bottles Nurse Jackson told me to place them around our patient's plastered leg.

"Now tell me why we do this, Nurse," she said.

"It helps dry the plaster," I told her promptly.

"And we need to keep the patient warm too, don't we?" Nurse Jackson said, tucking a blanket round him and directing me to put more bottles into the bed.

"Not too close, Nurse, in case you burn him," she said, turning and smiling at our patient.

"Is that all right?" I asked him anxiously.

"That's fine, miss," he said. "But I wish you could do something about this bed. It's awfully hard."

"I'm sorry about that," said Nurse Jackson, "but we must keep your leg straight. We don't want to make it worse, do we?" She turned to smile at me, one eyebrow raised. I smiled back. I like Nurse Jackson. Unlike some of the QAs she doesn't treat me as if I've never been on a ward before.

Just before going off duty I heard a cry behind the screen. "Oh, Nurse, stop. Please, stop!" a voice begged.

What was the matter with that patient? I wondered. He'd lain for several hours on hard boards and I was worried that his back was hurting him. I peeped round the screens. Nurse Jackson was tickling the motorcyclist's bare toes.

"Got to keep the circulation going, my lad," I heard her say to him, chuckling.

Wednesday 21 February

The strangest sound woke me last night – a sort of distant muffled thudding. But when I woke properly, the night was quiet again and I went back to sleep. Much later I woke again. This time I could hear vehicles – lots of them – driving up to the hospital. I padded over to the window, but of course I couldn't see anything because of the blackout shutters. Jean was still fast asleep.

In the morning I'd forgotten all about it. But when I went downstairs I noticed that the corridors were busier than usual, and everyone's faces looked drawn and very grim. Suddenly I remembered the noise that had woken me, and the vehicles I'd heard driving up to the hospital. I felt sure then that something awful must have happened, and I found myself trembling as I walked down the long corridor towards the Surgical ward.

I don't think anything could have prepared me for what I saw there.

The corridor was lined with men, lying, still in uniform, or bits of it, on stretchers. Dozens of them, all with dirty blackened faces and hair. Some of them stared blankly at me as I stepped carefully round them. Others just stared straight ahead unseeingly.

Slowly I pushed open the ward doors. I was dreading what I'd see inside.

If it had been bad in the corridor, this was even worse.

It was chaos. I saw MOs, masks on their faces, khaki sleeves rolled up, striding hastily from bed to bed. On the pillows lay faces black with dirt and oil. Burned arms, hands and legs lay still on the white sheets or under cradles. I saw a QA gently lift a man's burned arm to slip a towel underneath. Stuff oozed out. He didn't complain, though I could tell that it hurt him very much.

For a moment I stood there, swaying. I felt sick. I didn't feel as if I was in a hospital at all. The sight before me – it was what I imagined a field hospital at the Front to be like – except here we weren't being shot at. Then Nurse Jackson saw me. She took off her mask as she hurried up to me. A ship had been blown up by a floating mine in the Channel, she told me quickly. All those men who'd been picked up had been taken to the nearest hospitals. A lot of them had been brought here, I thought. As I looked around the ward, I couldn't see any of the patients I'd nursed yesterday. What was I to do? I thought in a panic. I tried to concentrate on what Nurse Jackson was telling me.

"Heat up some hot-water bottles for me, will you, Nurse?" I heard her say. "We need to get the patients warm.

They're in shock," she explained. You can tell that from the look in their eyes – as though they're far away; as though they don't know where they are. I'd read that somewhere in my Red Cross Manual, or had I?

I don't know *anything* I thought humbly. I looked at the QAs. They looked calm and competent as they bent over their patients – and suddenly I felt so relieved that they were there. How dare *I* think of myself as a nurse?

Nurse Jackson's voice interrupted my thoughts.

"The surgeon can't treat them until *we've* treated the shock. We can't wash them – or even undress them. So jump to it, please, Nurse."

Afterwards I went round the ward, holding cups of water and sweet tea up to blistered lips. The ward doors slammed. Another man was being wheeled out to Theatre.

Nurse Jackson was dabbing gentian violet on to a man's badly burned chest. He'd come back from Theatre earlier and it had to be done three times a day. She was wearing a mask and in a whisper told me to put one on too. It protects the men from picking up germs from us – and us from the smell. The smell from our burned patients is terrible. But the look in their eyes – that's far worse.

I watched while she went round the room again, irrigating the men's eyes. Soon she was called to a desperately injured patient. She told me to take over.

"You know what to do now," she said briskly.

My hands were shaking as I held a kidney bowl under a man's cheek to stop liquid running down on to the sheets. I could hardly bear to look at his face. I mustn't funk it, I whispered to myself again and again. *I mustn't.*

I could see Jean, moving from bed to bed. She looked so calm – unlike me.

By the time I'd been round the ward once it was time to begin again. We were so busy that we couldn't stop to think about what was happening there – or anything else.

But when I left the ward it flooded over me. And now – reliving it again as I write my diary – I feel sick again. Jean told me that my face was green when I came off duty. "It's all right now – just a bit pale," she said, smiling tiredly at me and switching off the light. I tried to smile back, but I couldn't.

In just this one day I feel as if I've seen more suffering than most people see in a whole lifetime. The safe little cocoon I've been living in these last few months has been blown away. When I'd got back to my room I'd pulled out Giles's letter. I was thinking about him, but not just him – I was thinking about all the wounded sailors on our ward – and all the others, too. I could do so little for any of them, but somehow – by writing to Giles – I felt as if it was one more – tiny – thing I could do for them. Does that make any sense?

Thursday 22 February

It seemed only a few hours later that I was again manoeuvring my way down the corridor past the stretchers filled with wounded men. I was exhausted and I hadn't even started work yet. All night, scenes from that nightmare ward had played themselves over and over in my head.

Inside the ward, a QA was giving a patient sips of water from a cup. "Take over, please, Nurse," she said when she saw me. As I got near the bed that awful smell hit me. Trying to ignore it, I turned to smile at the patient. My smile stuck on my face.

It was awful!

His face was all wrong – burnt and twisted out of shape – as though a small child had tried to mould a face out of plasticine. I'd seen plenty of burned men yesterday, but this... I forced myself to smile, but it was a pretty feeble one.

"Hello, Nurse," he said to me slowly, his lips stretching painfully into something resembling a smile. His courage made me feel ashamed. I took the cup from the QA and sat down next to him.

I stayed at his side until the QA came back to fetch me. "We need more sterile towels, Nurse," she said briskly. "And then I'd like you to strip and make up the empty beds. Hurry up now!"

"Doesn't he need specialing?" I asked her timidly.

"Look about you, Nurse," she said sadly. "Every one of these boys needs special nursing."

As I was making up the beds, tucking grey blankets over the long, red mackintosh sheets, I wondered who'd been in them last. At that, my mind just shut down.

I feel such rage inside me now when I think about the War. I tell myself to try and live it down. Being angry won't help anyone. But it's awfully hard.

Saturday 24 February

Slept badly again last night. I dread getting up in the morning now. Each time I push open the ward doors I have to screw up all my courage. Some of the things I've seen these last days are too awful even to write in my diary. I haven't been able to talk to *anyone* about it. This morning, lying in bed, I felt worse still. I wanted to run away – leave it all behind. I wanted my life to go back to how it was before this awful war began. I just couldn't cope any more.

I could hear Jean thrashing around in bed, as though she couldn't sleep either.

I got up to open the blackout shutters and poked my head outside. I could see the sea shimmering in the early morning sun. When I turned round Jean was sitting up, rubbing her eyes. She gave me a smile, but I was sure she felt as bad as I did. I was about to say something when she said, "Good morning, Kitty", climbed out of bed and quickly and efficiently pulled out her nurse's uniform. I watched as deftly she made up a fresh cap. I got dressed, too, and hunted for my cap. I found it, lying on a box. I looked at it. I'd worn it for a few days but it would do for another one.

"Kitty, that cap's looking a bit sad. Let me make up another one for you." Jean pinned a fresh white cap on my hair. She handed me her mirror and I peered at it. The face that stared back at me wasn't the sad, drained face I'd expected to see. It looked tired but competent too under the crisply starched white cap. A nurse's face. Suddenly I felt a whole lot better.

Today was just another day for us VADs. I smiled at Jean – a really warm smile this time and we went downstairs together. Once I'd thought she was a cold fish. I couldn't have been more wrong.

Sunday 25 February

At about five o'clock this afternoon, Sister came up to me. She looked harassed.

"Ah, Nurse Langley," she said briskly. "Theatre's just rung and told me they need extra help. Would you go down there, please."

"What – me?" I gulped, looking round wildly for Jean. Surely Sister didn't mean me. I've had precious little Theatre training.

"Yes, you," said Sister briskly. "Run along now."

Jean was just entering the ward as I left. I threw her an anguished glance.

"What's up?" she whispered.

"I've got to go to Theatre!" I told her.

"Good luck!" she whispered.

In a bit of a daze I made my way down to the operating-theatre suite. All down the corridor were men, lying there on stretchers. Some of them looked in a pretty bad way. I tried not to look at their faces. One of them might soon be lying on the operating table in front of me.

Heart thudding in my chest, I marched into the

"scrubbing-up" room. I leaned over the sink and began to scrub my hands and arms up to my elbows. I wondered what they'd ask me to do. I was feeling terribly nervous and there was a sick feeling in my tummy.

Theatre Sister told me to get dressed quickly. I got into a theatre gown, and tied a cap on my head, making sure that every hair was tucked securely under it. Then I put on a mask and rubber gloves. My hands were trembling, and I saw Sister look at them.

"Are you all right?" she asked. "The last girl they sent us fainted."

I swallowed. I wished she hadn't said that. Holding my hands clasped in front of me, as we always do after we've washed our hands, so that I wouldn't touch anything that wasn't sterile, I followed her into Theatre.

My job was a simple one – to fetch and carry for the team. I stood by the wall and waited as the long minutes ticked by. I looked anywhere (and everywhere) but at the patient. There was Theatre Sister, standing next to the surgeon. There was another gowned figure nearby – the anaesthetist. My eyes wandered round the room, resting in turn on a lotion bowl in a tall stand, on an instrument table where the surgeon's instruments lay – I tried not to shudder as I looked at them – and then there were dressing trolleys, and a bucket where the dirty swabs were dropped. Every so often I saw the surgeon turn to Sister and ask her to pass him something – a swab or an instrument like a scalpel or probe to examine the wound. I tried not to listen as he bent over the patient. I tried to concentrate on something else – anything but what was happening to our patient. I mustn't faint, I told myself. I mustn't let the team down.

"We need sterile dressing towels, Nurse," a voice interrupted my thoughts. I shot off, heart thudding in my chest, to fetch them. And then suddenly it was all over and our patient was being wheeled out of Theatre. My job now – to rinse out the bloody dressing towels. Then finally it was *my* turn to wash. I looked down at myself. Rivulets of blood were dripping down my front. I really nearly did faint then.

Friday 8 March

We're less busy in Theatre now as most of our ship casualties have been evacuated to hospitals inland. I'd expected to be sent back to Surgical, but I've stayed on here. I thought Jean would be envious that I'm working in Theatre, but she says not.

Anyway, I spend most of my time merely washing

stuff in the sluice room. On a busy day, bucket after bucket of dirty towels is dumped at my feet. After they've been rinsed in cold water in the sluice – this helps to get the blood out – there are all the instruments to clean. First they have to be scrubbed and cleaned with metal polish, and only then are they sterilized. Theatre clothing needs to be sterilized too – this goes into the autoclave.

But today, I *was* asked to go into Theatre again. I was awfully pleased. I stood there for about an hour – and then all I had to do was hand the surgeon a towel!

Wednesday 13 March

Our Theatre was crowded this morning. The surgeon was trying out a new technique and the room was full of excited doctors. When I wasn't busy I stopped by to watch too.

One of the surgeons is very nice. He's quite friendly – a bit like nice Lieutenant Venables. When he's not too busy, he even tells me what he's doing. In Theatre, we're like a little family, and I actually miss it when I go off duty.

"You're joking!" Bunty said, shuddering when I told her. We were walking down to the tennis courts together, rackets swinging in our hands.

"There's lots of cleaning too, of course," I said. "That's mostly what I do. I'm not always needed in the operating theatre itself. Sometimes I wish I was back on the wards. I do miss the patients."

"At least your ones can't answer back," said Bunty, grinning.

"Bunty!" exclaimed Molly.

I laughed and lobbed a ball high into the air. "I was back in the operating theatre today," I told her.

"Don't tell me," said Molly shuddering, scurrying down to the far end of the court where Marjorie was waiting. "It was an amputation, I'll bet. I don't want to know."

"It was very interesting," I said, seriously. "The surgeon. . ." I stopped and lunged in vain for the ball, which was soaring high over my head.

"You're putting me off," Bunty said crossly, serving another ball wide of the court. It bounced at Molly's feet. Molly just stood there, looking at it. Even across the court I could see that her face looked odd. It was really green.

Monday 18 March

Early this morning Theatre Sister asked me to help her lay out the instruments for the first operation on the surgeon's list. I muddled through somehow.

"You'll soon learn," Sister said, smiling, as I ran off and came back with the wrong instrument – again. I can't think how she manages to remember it all.

After we'd finished the day's operations, she gave me a book to study. "This will help you," she said. "Study it well." I took the book from her. I must have looked awfully anxious, for she laughed. "Don't worry," she said. "I'll check that we have all the right instruments before we go into Theatre."

Feel very flattered that she thinks I'm worth training. On Sunday morning – Sundays are usually quiet as we don't often have any operations – she's going to give me a proper lesson.

Giles has won his pilot's wings! I had a letter from him today in which he told me all about it. He's a fully-fledged fighter pilot with Fighter Command's "11 Group" now. Apparently that's the group that covers south-east England. There are several groups, he told me – each covering a different part of Britain. He'll be flying Spitfires, and he sounds jolly proud. Tomorrow he's going to join his squadron – and is longing to get a shot at the enemy. What is it about men? They spend all their time fighting, and then *we* have to patch them up!

Friday 5 April

Everyone here has been very buoyed up by the Prime Minster's speech. It seems he thinks that the Germans should have attacked us straightaway when the British and French armies weren't ready for them. Now, he believes, the situation's changed – our armies are much stronger now. I hope he's right.

This evening a call was put through from Father. I was thrilled! I haven't spoken to him since Boxing Day. He sounded guarded when I asked him what he thought about the Prime Minister's speech, but I'm going to try not to let his caution worry me.

Wednesday 10 April

The Germans have overrun Denmark and now they've invaded Norway. Norway is a neutral country – not on one side or the other in the conflict. But the Germans don't seem to care about that. It seems incredible but in only two days all the main Norwegian ports have been captured by the Germans.

The whole of Europe is being dragged into this terrible war. Too depressed to write any more.

Monday 15 April

Just as I'm learning to set the instrument table, I've been shifted back to the Surgical ward. Typical!

Today a plane crashed near the hospital. It was so close that all the glass rattled in the window panes. It was very hot in the ward and I'd just gone over to the windows to open one of them when I saw a long tail of black smoke vanish somewhere behind the trees and then suddenly there was a huge explosion. I felt very scared – and a bit sick. How could anyone survive that crash?

For what seemed like an age there was complete silence – then suddenly there was a dash for the windows. From his bed Private Jones swore blind that it was a Jerry plane. Over in his bed Corporal Lister was sceptical. "You couldn't even see the thing," he said. The Private said he just knew, but I could see that his eyes were twinkling. After that there was a lot of argy-bargying back and forth. Some of the men sided with Lister, others with Jones. In the midst of all this, Sister came in to do her round, looking as calm as if nothing had happened.

"What's going on in here?" she asked.

"Nothing, Sister. Sorry, Sister." And off they shuffled, looking sheepish.

Funnily enough, Private Jones was right – it was a Jerry plane. I know because the pilot was brought into the ward just before I went off duty this evening. He's our first prisoner of war. He was very quiet, and seemed rather frightened, and I found myself feeling sorry for him. It must be awful to be shot down in an enemy country and find yourself in a hospital ward surrounded by the very people you're fighting.

None of the aircrew have been brought in, so we think

they must have bought it. None of us know what that plane was doing here either.

Later on I had another thought. That plane could so easily have hit the hospital. There's a big red cross painted on the roof so that the enemy will know that we're a hospital and won't target us. But how will *that* protect us if a plane crashes on top of us, or a bomb misses its target and lands on us instead? I feel very scared when I think about that.

Tuesday 16 April

The men don't seem to mind sharing their ward with a German prisoner of war.

"Johannes's all right... He's just another poor lad – fighting for his country like the rest of us," one of them told me. I think they feel sorry for him – he's broken both his legs. And he'll be sent off to prisoner-of-war camp as soon as he's recovered.

Johannes seems a bit bewildered by us. He told me that he broke his legs in the fall and when he came round he saw a man pointing a gun at him. "I told him not to shoot. I said I wasn't armed," he said. Then, he said, a woman came out of the house near where he'd landed, a cup of hot, sweet tea in her hand. "She said it was for me." He shook his head. "I do not understand you English," he said.

Wednesday 1 May

I wish I knew what was happening across the Channel. News does reach us in the hospital, but sometimes it's hard to know *what* to believe – the rumours flying round the hospital or the news on the wireless. There've been a lot of angry mutters about how the government is handling the campaign in Norway. Our troops were sent out to help Norway in April – but they were ill-equipped and unprepared for the task they had to do apparently. No match for the Germans or the snow. I am *so* relieved that Peter isn't out there.

Friday 10 May

Jerry's invaded the Low Countries! We're all so shocked – everyone's walking around in a daze. First their airfields, railways and arms depots were bombarded from the air. Then the enemy's tanks rolled across the Dutch, Belgian and Luxembourg borders without warning. German planes are raining bombs down on their cities. Our Allied armies have been taken completely by surprise.

I'm writing this very late, but I had to get this down. Mr Chamberlain, our Prime Minister, has resigned! People haven't been at all happy about the way he's been running the War. Another minister, Mr Winston Churchill, is now our Prime Minister. At nine o'clock this evening we all crowded round the wireless in the VADs' mess to hear Mr Chamberlain's resignation broadcast to the nation. Mr Churchill went to the palace at 6 o'clock this evening to see the King, who's asked him to form a new government. There was a real sense of relief in the room.

"We'll be all right now," I heard someone say after we'd turned off the wireless. Oh, I pray they're right. There's something about Mr Churchill that makes us feel safe. He won't take any nonsense from Jerry, I feel sure, but is there anything anyone can do to help us now?

Thursday 16 May

The German army seems unstoppable. In the last few days they've stormed through neutral Belgium and now their tanks are rolling across France. They entered France through the Ardennes, an area in eastern France. That was another big surprise. The Ardennes region is hilly and forested, and it was thought that their tanks wouldn't be able to cross it. But apparently the Germans have got a new sort of tank, which seems able to cope with all sorts of obstacles – even forests and hills. The French armies are being pushed back under the German onslaught. The British Expeditionary Force is still standing its ground, but how much longer will it be able to do so?

Trying not to think what this means for us, but we're all jolly frightened.

Holland has surrendered to the Germans. As soon as I came off duty, I wrote at once to Peter and Giles. I don't know if my letter will ever reach Peter. I don't know if I will ever see him again. I cannot bear it.

Tuesday 21 May

When I woke up this morning I thought for an instant that I could hear something – guns, or bombs – a sort of distant boom, boom – far away, across the sea. I told myself not to be so silly, we can't possibly hear them here, and anyway, the Germans are still very far away, but I could feel my heart beat a lot faster.

I popped outside on my break. Shielding my eyes in the sun, I looked out to sea. You can't walk on the beach now. It's been mined and there's barbed wire draped everywhere – even on the promenades we used to cycle down.

Mr Churchill says we're in deep trouble. We've nothing to match the Jerry tanks. If the *Prime Minister* says that, then we are indeed in an awful fix.

Bit by bit, the British and French armies are being pushed back towards the sea. Nothing they do seems to be able to stop the German advance. I wish I could stop thinking about that. My brother's out there in that hell.

Wednesday 22 May

Letter from Mother today. She writes that she's made up her mind and joined ARP (Air Raid Precautions) – as an air-raid warden! She misses having us all to look after, she says, and she needs to feel she's doing something useful. Now it seems she's got a whole village on her hands!

She didn't mention Peter, so I know that she must be very worried about him. I wish I could go and see her but a lot of new patients are expected here soon and more VADs are being drafted in to help. It would be wonderful if Anne was amongst them!

Friday 24 May

On the 20th the Germans captured the French towns of Amiens and Abbeville. Our armies are retreating. At the hospital we're all holding our breath.

I'm trying not to think about the War. It is such a relief

to be able to bury myself in work. But as soon as I go off duty, I start to worry again. I can see worry plain on everyone else's faces, too. It's all anyone can talk about – what's going to happen now? Bunty's going round with a face as white as a sheet. The strain we're all under here is quite awful.

Sunday 26 May

Half day off – I spent it in Surgical. It's all hands to the deck now. All leave's been cancelled. Sister and our MO were kept busy all morning, doing rounds and organizing patients' discharges. For me it was back and forth to the store, returning hospital "blues" and bringing back the soldiers' kits. As I ran back and forth, I saw men in khaki and women, white caps on their heads – doctors and nurses I've never seen before. I don't know what they're doing here.

All those patients well enough to travel are being evacuated to hospitals further inland to make room for the new arrivals. They'll travel by ambulance train, escorted by a team of MOs and nurses. I still don't know who the new patients are, or why so many are expected here. But something's happened. Something big.

Monday 27 May

There are men lying on the floor, all along the corridor and in the ward, and on mattresses between the beds. Sweat pours off their faces, and they're filthy. As I entered I saw a VAD on her knees, cutting off a man's uniform. Her face was white and strained. It was Marjorie! I could see a dirty bandage swathed round the man's leg and there was an identity tag round his neck. It was unreadable – stained with blood and dirt. One of the QAs took me over to another stretcher. Under the blanket the man was fully dressed. She asked me to wash his face. "Do it gently, Nurse," she said. "And be quick about it. There are plenty more here that need washing."

I knelt on the floor by the stretcher, a bowl of warm water to hand. Gently I lifted the soldier's head, pillowing it on my arm, and began to wipe his face. His eyes were bloodshot and sweat was pouring off him.

"Wha... a... a... a..." he started to say. Oily stuff dribbled out of his mouth. I laid his head carefully back down on the stretcher. There was something staining my arm where his head had lain. I ran for help.

It was the last thing he said.

I ran into the annexe and leaned over the sink, taking deep breaths. I felt awful – too upset even for tears. Desperately I tried to pull myself together. *I've got to cope – everyone else is. I must cope. I must.*

"Nurse, I need your help," I heard a voice say gently behind me. I dried my face quickly and turned round. The QA had a stack of hot-water bottles in her arms. "Heat these up for me, will you?" she asked.

"The men. . ." I faltered. "I'm supposed to wash them."

"Never mind about that now. Nurse Mason's doing it."

Jean? I thought vaguely. She was working nights. *Was she still on duty?*

As soon as the men are brought in, the QAs and MOs go from mattress to bed, from bed to mattress. They check the men's breathing and pulse. Is that man still in shock? Can we risk removing his uniform? They call me over. "Nurse, I'd like you to wash this man, please." I run over and cut off his uniform as I've been shown. "Be careful how you do it, Nurse. We must try to save all we can." Gently I wash the gritty sand and dirt off him. Under an old bandage there's a wound on his abdomen. Blood is seeping through the bandage. I need a fresh bandage – now! The haemorrhage is staunched, the new bandage wound tightly over the wound.

"His pulse is very weak, Sister." I look up from my

patient at Sister's face. Sister's sleeves are rolled up. She looks as if she's been up all night.

An MO takes over and I'm sent to fill up hot-water bottles again. Soon, we've run out. "Nurse, look in the patients' beds – over there, Nurse, over there!" Blankly, I pull out a hot-water bottle from next to a patient's feet. The feet are very cold, I tell the Sister. He's dead, she says briskly. No time for tears here. The body is rolled into a blanket and lifted off the bed. Automatically I wash down the mackintosh sheet, dry it, and then I rip open a package and pull out another blanket, which I lay on top of it. Next to me the stretcher bearers are waiting impatiently. As soon as I've finished, the bed is filled again.

Back and forth I go into the annexe, squeezing out the flannel, watching dirt and blood and sweat swirl away together down the sluice.

QAs run round the ward and the corridors, handing out injections of morphia as though they're cups of tea. There are metal stands between the beds, bottles of blood swinging off them. Rubber tubes connect them to our patients.

A Sister asks me to sort through a pile of bloodstained clothing and get it ready to go off to the store. I'm glad to be able to keep my head down. Glad not to have to look for a time at those exhausted despairing faces, those blank eyes. But I can't shut out the groans, the eternal tramp

tramp tramp of the stretcher bearers, bringing more men into the ward, and taking others down to Theatre.

And still the ambulances come. The BEF is being evacuated from Dunkirk. When I first heard the news, I felt strangely relieved. Soon, I hoped, my brother would be home.

Not now.

Each time an ambulance arrives I wonder if he'll be amongst its patients. Each time the doors swing open, I have to force myself not to look up. I'm terrified. I don't want to see Peter here, but even worse is thinking of him left behind in France.

A cheerful, smiling nurse can do more to help her patients than a cross and weary one, I suddenly remember from my training. But I cannot laugh, I cannot smile. And oh, I am weary. And this – I feel horribly certain – is only the beginning.

Wednesday 29 May

Dragged myself up to bed at last at *three in the morning* – felt like curling up on the stairs – legs so wobbly and weak. Scribbling this in bed ... too tired to think...

That's some little comfort, I suppose. I must write my diary because I promised Anne. But I don't want to. I don't want to *remember* what I've seen today. I want to *forget*. I daren't let myself think – if I stop to think, I'll never get through this.

Thursday 30 May

We've had another blow. The Belgian army have surrendered to the Germans. It happened two days ago, I'm told. In the hospital the wards are overflowing. All our usual routine's gone to the winds, though Sister tries her best to keep order.

Though I'm constantly exhausted, I often wake up when the ambulances drive up to the hospital. It's hot and stuffy in our little room, too, which makes it hard to sleep, but we're not supposed to open the blackout shutters. Tonight, though, I felt I just couldn't breathe. I had to open the window. I crept quietly over to it and managed to prise it open. I gulped in the cool night air.

It was a clear night and I looked up at the stars. Those same stars shine over France, I found myself thinking, and then, without any warning, the tears came. I just stood there, trying not to sob, feeling the tears slide down my cheeks. Oh, please – don't let him be killed. Please.

I heard the door open and a moment later I felt a hand touch my shoulder. Jean had come in.

"What's wrong?" she asked. I couldn't speak. "Is it Peter?" she whispered. I nodded and felt her arm go round my shoulder. "Has anything happened to him?" she asked carefully.

"I don't know," I said. "I just don't know."

Jean stared out into the night. "My brother's out there too," she said.

"Oh, Jean," I said. "I'm so sorry." I put my arm round her shoulders and we stood there, the tears silently pouring down our cheeks.

Friday 31 May

As soon as I arrived on the ward this morning one of the QAs hurried up to me. She took me over to a bed surrounded by screens.

"I'd like you to keep an eye on this boy while I find an MO." She lowered her voice. "He's very sick."

I looked at my charge. His eyes had opened ever so

slightly when he heard our voices. Now he closed them again. I saw what an effort even this took. He looked awfully young – younger even than Peter. There was a blanket on the bed and though it was quite warm in the room, he was shivering. I took his hand in mine and rubbed his fingers gently, trying to warm them. They were very cold. I asked him his name, but it was clearly too difficult for him to speak. I talked gently to him. I don't know what I said exactly but soon I forgot everything else – all the chaos and the noise on the other side of the screens. Occasionally I saw him move his lips slightly – they looked awfully dry, so I got up and dampened them with a moistened swab.

My patient's lips were moving again and I leaned over the bed to listen. A smell – that awful stench of dried blood that I know so well now – rose up from the bed and it was all I could do not to retch. "Thank you," I heard him murmur faintly. And then he said something else and I leaned closer to hear. "Billy." His voice sounded as if it were coming from somewhere far away.

"Billy, I'm Kitty," I whispered, close to his ear. I didn't care that it was against the rules to tell him my name. It couldn't matter now. I squeezed his fingers, very gently. Billy's face was very pale and stained with perspiration, and I could see something damp begin to seep through the red army blanket. The wound had begun to bleed again.

I stood up urgently. Where was the MO? I needed help – now. And then I heard a sigh and there was a sudden movement under the blanket – a sort of shudder that seemed to pass through Billy's whole body. I was still holding his hand.

A screen was moved aside. The MO was standing there, the QA next to him. The MO leaned over the boy and took his stiffening wrist loosely in his hand. It's too late for that, I thought. I was trying to choke back tears. Quietly I got to my feet and made myself walk across the ward to the annexe. I didn't want anyone to see my tears.

The QA caught up with me a few minutes later. She asked me to wash the bedstead and change the sheets. I didn't need to look back to know that the screens had gone and the body lifted off the bed. How could she ask this of me? I wondered dully. A boy had just died in that bed. Didn't she care? "His name was Billy," I wanted to tell her. I felt angry and upset. And then – fleetingly – I saw the sadness deep in the QA's eyes, and the tiredness, and I felt ashamed.

I made up poor Billy's bed. I don't know how I did it, but I did.

Saturday 1 June

Wounded soldiers are pouring in from the Front in France each day. Here, days and nights run into each other, but I'm thankful that I'm able to do something useful. New VADs arrived again today from outstations – sick bays, first-aid posts and other hospitals. I keep hoping to see Anne's merry face amongst them, but I've heard nothing more about her hoped-for transfer.

Whenever I have time to grab a break, I go outside – stepping through corridors packed with wounded men, all of them waiting to be admitted. I take off my mask and breathe deeply – filling my lungs with fresh air, glad to get rid of the hospital smell. Today I sat down for a time on the warm grass, under the shade of a big sycamore tree. While I was sitting there, a squirrel bounded across the lawn in front of me. It stopped and looked at me and I looked back at it. Then it was off again, running up the tree. That squirrel doesn't know we're at war, I thought suddenly. Its life carries on as it always has. The thought comforted me a little. I looked out to sea again. There was a great ship bobbing up and down in the Channel, nose pointed to port. I wondered if it was a hospital ship, bringing more of the wounded home. It was like a signal to me. Tiredly I got to my feet and made my way back to the ward.

Only the very sickest are brought to coastal hospitals like ours. They're a motley lot – they come from regiments stationed all over the country. Some of them had their wounds dressed in France or on board ship on the way home, but even so, infection can set in. There's not much we can do if it really takes hold. I hate feeling so helpless.

Sunday 2 June

This morning I was asked to wash a new patient. Like all our new arrivals his face was caked with dirt. He had a shrapnel wound and I knew that he'd soon be going to Theatre. As I washed the dirt off him, I saw his eyes on me, grimacing with pain. I felt distressed. I asked if I was hurting him.

"I'm all right, Nurse," he said shortly. "Don't bother about me," his eyes seemed to be saying. "Don't bother about any of us. We're not worth it." There was such shame on his face.

Gradually I've begun to understand why. Our boys lost the battle and they feel that they've let us down. But to us they're heroes and I cannot begin to imagine what they've had to endure. I hope that they'll understand this soon.

Monday 3 June

There have been a lot of mutters about the RAF. "Where were the RAF when we needed them?" This is all one poor boy says. Everyone who walks past his bed gets asked the same question. "Where were the RAF?" Just that. Again and again. Sometimes he screams in his sleep. It upsets the other patients, but we can't move him, as there's nowhere for him to go. Another patient told me that they were bombarded by enemy planes as they retreated. They didn't just target soldiers, he said, but refugees as well. Old people, children – it made no difference. Jerry planes strafed the lot. We could do nothing for them, he said. Our planes were nowhere to be seen. I could see that his eyes were swimming as he relived the horror of the memory, and I went to fetch him a cup of tea. My legs were shaking as I walked over to the ward kitchen. I thought I'd heard and seen it all, but the soldier's words sickened me. What kind of person does a thing like that?

It was growing dark, and I put up the blackout boards. I still couldn't put that soldier's words out of my mind. Where had the RAF been, I wondered. I hoped that Giles would be able to tell me.

I don't know what time it was when I went off duty. I hadn't eaten anything since lunch, but I couldn't have touched a morsel.

Jean came in when I was still sitting on the bed, too tired even to get undressed. She had two mugs of Ovaltine in her hands. I looked at her drained face. It seemed to reflect what I was feeling. I took one of the mugs gratefully in my cold and shaking hands. "Nurse Mason," I said to her. "What would I do without you?"

Tuesday 4 June

Mr Winston Churchill, the Prime Minister, has spoken to the nation. It was a wonderful speech. We crowded round the wireless to listen. I managed to scribble down some of what he said.

"We shall fight on the beaches, we shall fight on

the landing-grounds, we shall fight in the fields and in the streets, we shall fight in the hills; we shall never surrender."

Feel tearful, proud and full of renewed hope and purpose. Whenever I feel despondent, I will look at these words. I don't merely hope we'll win any more. I *know* we will.

Thursday 6 June

In his speech the Prime Minister also said that the RAF played a big part in helping the British and French armies escape from Dunkirk. I'd heard that German bombers targeted the towns and beaches where the men were waiting and the ships sent to pick up the men. They even bombed hospital ships! And Dunkirk and other French coastal towns nearby have been bombed into blazing ruins. But without the RAF, the Prime Minister says, the situation would have been even worse. There were a few disbelieving snorts amongst our patients when they learnt what he'd said. And today I heard them muttering about it again. I was accompanying some of them down to the station where they were to catch an ambulance train. As we bumped down the drive, a young boy with a bandaged head said: "Our Prime Minister's just covering up for them – RAF cowards."

"Only planes *I* saw had those black-and-white crosses on them," snorted another, who'd lost an eye. "Since when did our planes have black-and-white crosses on them?"

There were more angry snorts. I just sat there silently. I felt sure they were wrong, or were they? After all, they had been there, hadn't they? As I looked at them – at their injuries – I thought they had every right to be bitter. So this evening I sat down at last and wrote to Giles. I know it may be weeks before I hear from him, but I've at least got to try and find out what really happened at Dunkirk.

Monday 10 June

Mother rang today. Peter is home! Not wounded, not dead – he's safe. He's exhausted, Mother said when she finally got put through to me. Otherwise he's all right – and very relieved to be back. Mother says he was picked up in a little boat – that there were hundreds of them helping the soldiers get off the beaches. Whoever picked Peter up saved my brother's life. I don't know who you are but thank you, thank you, thank you.

Tuesday 11 June

All down one side of the ward now are men with arms or legs encased in plaster – bones shattered by gunshot or shrapnel. It's horrible, the smell that comes off them. When I go over to them, I try not to let my face show that I notice it, but they know. Poor boys, it's so much worse for them. We've tried all sorts of things to hide that smell, but nothing works.

Italy declared war on us yesterday.

Monday 17 June

France has surrendered. Now we are really on our own. It may sound odd, but in a way I feel relieved. At least now we know where we stand. Jean's awfully worried. She thinks that her brother's still in France, but she's not had any news of him. She doesn't know if he's been captured, or even if he's still alive.

We sat together in the VADs' mess, aching feet propped up on chairs, mugs of hot tea in our hands. Bunty was looking so pale. I wish I knew if she's heard from her officer, but I feel too scared to ask. Lots of people are going round the hospital with that same look on their faces – people who've lost brothers, husbands or sons at Dunkirk. We didn't talk much – we were all too tired – and I fell asleep in my chair. When I woke up, they'd gone and the half-full mug was still in my hand.

I don't know how I find the energy to keep up my diary, but I don't know what I'd do without it. Sometimes I can't bear to relive my day, and it's only my promise to Anne that makes me write. But at other times it brings me comfort of a sort.

Thursday 20 June

Ambulances full of wounded men arrived here yesterday. The operating theatres are working flat out again and I was told to report there this morning. One after another the men were wheeled in with awful gunshot or shrapnel wounds. Then it's back on to the wards again, a few hours later, often with one bit or another missing.

So many shattered or gangrenous limbs that can't be saved.

The last of our forces are being brought back from France. They'd retreated west of Dunkirk to the Cherbourg peninsula. But Jean still has no news of her brother. I feel so grieved for her.

We went out for a walk together this evening. We hadn't gone far when we saw the oddest sight – fields full of old cars. Apparently it's to stop German planes from landing in them. Everyone expects that the Germans will try and invade us soon. All there is to stop them now is a thin stretch of water – and the RAF. But if the worst happens our boys will be ready for them and we are relieved that so many have got safely out of France.

Friday 21 June

I got a letter from Giles today. He did take part in the "battle for France". He says he doesn't think the Germans will risk an invasion until they've destroyed our air force and have control of the air. And there was something else, which made me sit up.

"I'm glad you asked me about Dunkirk," he wrote.

"People here seem very angry with the RAF. They don't even try to listen to our side of things and I want to set the record straight. To put it bluntly, if we'd not been there, many of our boys would still be holed up in France, either dead or in a German prisoner-of-war camp. I guess the lads on the ground didn't see us, but we were there all right."

In his letter he said that he'd made many sorties to France. "Once," he said, "I really thought I'd bought it – engine ran out of petrol. I had just enough fuel left to get me back over the Channel but I had to make an emergency landing in a field and find my own way back to base."

I felt very thoughtful as I put the letter away. So my patients had been wrong and the Prime Minister was right. Giles should be very proud of what he did. He sounds different somehow – older, grown up. If only I could feel more for him, but I just can't.

Sunday 23 June

As soon as I got off duty today I collapsed into bed. I woke up again when Jean came in. She had two mugs of hot tea in her hands, and there was a huge smile on her face. Most unJean-like! Sleepily I sat up in bed.

"All right, tell," I said, patting the bed next to me. She flopped down on the bed at once. I'd guessed what she was going to say, for she looked so happy.

Her brother got out on one of the last ships to leave Cherbourg, she told me, beaming. German tanks harried them all the way to the port. She shivered and I gave her a big hug. I can't begin to imagine what it must have been like – and then I thought about the dirty, exhausted faces of the wounded men pouring into the hospital, and I wondered about those others, the ones who didn't get out.

There are a lot of Poles among our patients now. We all know how brave they were and how they refused to surrender to the enemy when it looked as if it was all up for them. Somehow they managed to reach the French coast and were brought safely across the Channel to Britain. There's a rumour that as many as 20,000 of them have got away!

In spite of everything there's a good atmosphere in the country, and it's rubbing off on us in the hospital. One of the QAs told me that as well as the Poles, Czechs, Canadians, Free French, New Zealanders, Australians and South Africans, and many from other lands too, are flooding into the country to join our forces! *Not* that we needed anything more to stiffen our resolve.

So many acts of heroism and courage. Big ones and

little ones. I see them every day in both our patients and staff. This war brings out all that's best in us. It doesn't matter what the enemy does, I *know* that somehow we will come through this. We must.

Friday 28 June

When I went off duty today, the first person I saw was Bunty. She looked very drawn and tired. She smiled at me, but her eyes were sad. She seemed to be making an effort to hold on to herself. She told me she had something to tell me and together we went into the VADs' mess. I felt scared. What was she going to tell me? Had something happened to her officer?

We sat down. I waited.

"It was awful on the ward today," she said at last. Her voice was barely a whisper. "You cannot imagine how awful." Her lips trembled and I was afraid that she was going to break down. I felt shocked. I didn't recognize the Bunty I knew in this sad and shaken girl. So this was what she wanted to tell me. That she couldn't cope. Bunty! Of all people! I put my hands on her shoulders and shook her slightly. She looked surprised. Then I surprised myself.

"Bunty," I said, firmly. "You've got to pull yourself together. It's the same for all of us."

She turned away from me, laying her head on her arm. "You've changed, Kitty. You sound so – so *hard*."

I flinched. "I'm only trying to help," I said. I felt so hurt.

"Oh, Kitten, I can't bear it any more," she burst out suddenly. I looked at her, startled.

She looked up at me, eyes brimming now. "I always used to dread it when the wounded were brought in, in case it was him, but today . . . each time a wounded man came on to the ward, I hoped and prayed it *would* be him, that he's just wounded . . . not . . . not. . ."

She began to sob and suddenly I felt cold all through. "He . . . he's never coming back. Oh, Kitty, he's been killed!"

I stroked her hair until her sobs had died down. "Bunty, I'm so sorry," I whispered. Tears were running down my face now. I wish I'd listened to her when she'd tried to tell me. I wish I hadn't been so hard on her.

Saturday 29 June

As soon as I finished work today I got out my bicycle. Soon I was out in the countryside, pedalling hard.

I was still feeling upset about what I'd said to Bunty – and what she'd said to me. Had I changed? I admired the way professional nurses coped, and somehow I'd also found the strength to cope. But had I become harder too?

I hadn't, had I? I thought desperately.

I cycled until I felt too tired to cycle any more. On the way back to the hospital I saw a radar tower facing out to sea. I remembered what Peter had once told me about them – how they help us track down enemy planes – and I took a good look at it as I cycled past.

Suddenly I hit a stone and my tyre blew. Bother, I thought. I hopped off, and pulled out my repair kit.

I was still fumbling with it rather hopelessly when I heard a voice call out and a bicycle pulled up next to me. It was Lieutenant Venables! Was I relieved to see him! He took my kit from me and I stood by and watched as he deftly fixed the puncture.

When he stood up again, his hands were covered in

sticky black oil and there was a smudge on his cheek. I saw that he was about to put his oily hands into his pockets so I quickly fished out a hanky and gave it to him. It was the sort of thing Peter would do, I found myself thinking as, rather sheepishly, he wiped his oily cheek and hands.

Together, we cycled back up to the hospital. I told him I was working in Theatre again and he asked me how I liked it. "I'd rather be on the wards." I told him. He smiled at me as if he understood. By the time we'd got back I was feeling a whole lot happier. I do like Lieutenant Venables. Later I found myself thinking about him again. It'd been such a long time since I'd seen him. And then I remembered Bunty and I felt ashamed that I could have forgotten her troubles so easily, and I went off to find her. Honestly, I'm heartless, I really am.

Thursday 18 July

Letter from Anne today. "It sounds simply awful down there," she wrote. "Poor Kitten, I do feel so worried about you and all our friends. Please write soon and let me know that you're all right.

"You know that transfer I've been trying to get? Well,

you'll never guess what the wretched army's gone and done now! It's posting me still further away – to a sick bay attached to a barracks in some deserted spot.

"It's not fair! Here I am, hockey stick at the ready, desperate to come and help you defend our island against the Jerries. Ah well . . . write soon?

"PS: I hope you're writing your diary, as promised. I am! But then, I have precious little else to do in my off-duty time. I don't suppose you've been having much of that."

I feel sad to think that Anne won't be transferring here. I feel a bit guilty, too. I haven't been keeping up my diary as I should. I haven't felt like writing at all. Oh, Anne, I hope you'll forgive me.

Saturday 20 July

I went down to the station this morning. It was my first whole day off in a very long time and I was planning to spend it at home. I was in heaven at the prospect of getting right away from the hospital, even if it was just for a day.

I stood on the platform and waited. At last the train came – a whole hour late! When we chugged into the station at last, I knew I'd have to hurry to catch my connection – and I tore across the platform. As I leaped down the stairs two at a time, I saw the train pull out of the station. There wasn't another train for a very long time, so all I could do was wait and catch the next train back to the hospital. I felt so upset. I'd been looking forward to going home. Mother had written that Peter was home on leave. And for once Father would be at home, too. I haven't seen any of them since New Year.

I scrounged a lift back up to the hospital. Then I went to find the others. Molly was off duty too, and we cycled out into the countryside together. We rode up and down country lanes, and then we stopped at a pub and I blew nearly a whole week's wages on the best meal I'd had since New Year.

It was nearly dark when we climbed back on to our bicycles and we had to cycle really slowly. It's easy to get lost now, as there are no streetlights to guide you, and all the signposts have been taken down to confuse the enemy.

Suddenly Molly clutched my arm and we both wobbled and nearly fell off our bikes. In a loud whisper she told me she'd heard a noise – a sort of rustling in one of the hedges.

"It's probably just a rabbit or a mouse," I told her, sounding braver than I felt. Then Molly started to tell me about the Jerry spies who've been seen parachuting into southern England. Feeling really scared now, I asked her how she knew. Well, then she told me that they've been seen in the town – disguised as nuns! I felt so relieved that I began to laugh. There have been a lot of invasion scares and rumours, but this was just *too* silly. Molly, I think, felt a bit peeved but then she saw the funny side too. Our laughter sounded most peculiar out there in the dark, so we got hastily back on our bikes and cycled on.

It was late when at last we crept up to the hospital, wheeling our bikes. The door was locked but we squeezed in through a ground-floor window that someone had forgotten to close. We couldn't stop giggling as we tiptoed down the darkened corridors and up the stairs. What a day!

Sunday 21 July

Hitler's offered to make peace with Britain! We won't have any of it of course. Peace would mean surrendering all we've been fighting for. We're fighting on.

A trunk call was put through from Mother today. The line was crackling badly, but she managed to ask how I was. I told her I was fine. The crackles got worse. "What did you say?" I asked. I was practically bawling into the phone now. It was something about the enemy bombing the coastal towns. Even through the crackles I could hear the panic in her voice. The town has been hit, but I didn't tell her. Hitler's planes are attacking our shipping, too. I told her not to worry about me, and then I asked how she was, and Father and Peter. It was a while before I realized that the line had gone dead.

Wednesday 24 July

I had the oddest dream yesterday. I dreamed that a plane flew down low – so low that I could even see the pilot's face. It was Giles. I called to him but he couldn't hear me. He could see me though. He smiled and waved. Three times he circled the hospital, each time his plane getting higher and higher. Then off he flew into the clouds, with me still calling vainly after him, the way you do in dreams.

When I woke up I felt very out of sorts. I told myself that it had just been a dream, that probably there'd been planes flying past as I'd slept. But I couldn't stop worrying and I told myself I'd write to Giles as soon as I finished my shift. I didn't though. I was so tired when I came off duty this morning – I'm back on nights again now – that I just collapsed into bed. Tomorrow though I *will* write to Giles. I haven't heard from him since he wrote to me about Dunkirk. I must write back and tell him that I understand better now.

Saturday 27 July

Peter scooted over to see me today. I can't think how he managed to wangle the petrol for the trip. It was wonderful to see him. He told me he felt he had to keep an eye on me – he thought I'd spun a story about the train! We rode out into the countryside, me clinging tightly to his back. It was a bit of a squash. I looked a fright when we arrived at the inn – my hair stuck up all over the place.

After we'd finished our meal he asked me about my work. "You were in the thick of it, weren't you, Sis?"

I doodled with the spoon in my saucer before answering. I knew that he was thinking about Dunkirk but I didn't want to talk about it. "Yes," I said shortly. "But most of the time I was too busy to think about it."

"I know," he said, staring straight ahead of him. "It was a bit like that for me. But now – now I wish I could forget."

His eyes looked very far away – as if he was back on the beaches at Dunkirk. Why was I spared? Why me when so many weren't? I could see the thought plain on his face. I tried to bring him back.

"We all have to find our own way through this," I said. "We have to show them we're not beaten. We can't give up, or they've won."

Peter didn't say anything for a long time. He still seemed very far away. And then he told me how one night they'd made their way down to the beach and waded out to sea. How they'd stood in the icy water, hoping to get picked up by one of the little ships bobbing up and down in the waves – each man for himself. I stopped him then.

"What little ships?" And then dimly I remembered that Mother had said something about the little ships when she told me how Peter had got back to England, and hadn't the Prime Minister also said something about them in his broadcast to us?

Peter looked very surprised. "Didn't you know?" he asked.

"Tell me," I said.

Peter drew in breath. "Everyone who owned a boat on the south-east coast was asked to take it over to France. There were all sorts," he said. "Some quite small – even fishing boats. The troop carriers couldn't get in near enough to pick us up. There was nowhere for them to berth, as all the piers that were any use had been destroyed by Jerry bombers. So the little boats had to ferry us between the beaches and the ships. They made trip after trip." He shook his head wonderingly. "Those chaps were amazing. We'd never have got away without them. Even then, it was a bit of a scramble." His face darkened again.

I imagined the pushing and shoving, as the men fought for a seat in one of the little boats – their only passport to safety. I shuddered.

"All the time there were those silver wings wheeling and diving overhead. They weren't seagulls, Kitty," Peter said, giving a lopsided smile. "They were planes – Jerry planes. We were sitting ducks," he added. "The night I got out – think it was night. Hard to tell – there was a big, black smoky cloud over everything much of the time – we were being bombed all the time, you see. Anyway, when I got out, Dunkirk was blazing so Jerry could see us beautifully, even at night. Picked men out of the sea like fishes. Rat-a-tat-tat," he said, imitating the noise of the planes' guns as they fired on the men. He stopped again, lost in the memory.

"How's Giles?" he said suddenly. There was a touch of bitterness in his voice. RAF pilots, it seemed to say, easy ride *they* had. I remembered what Giles had written in his last letter. I wanted to tell Peter, but there was such anger in his face that I just didn't know if he'd believe me. And I didn't want to row about it and spoil the evening.

"I don't know," I said slowly, answering his question. "I don't really care any more, but I don't know how to tell him."

Peter nodded thoughtfully. "Probably best not to – at least not right now," he said. He stood up. "You're on duty tonight, aren't you? I'd better get you back."

After he'd dropped me off, I hugged him tightly. "Take care of yourself, Pete," I whispered. He had one foot already on the pedal. He flashed a smile up at me.

"You know, we haven't quarrelled this evening – not once," he said. "Must be a record." I felt relieved that I'd not brought up the subject of the RAF's role at Dunkirk.

The twins wanted to know who Peter was. I'd seen them hanging out of the window as we rode back up to the hospital. I told them he was my brother, but I don't think they believed me.

"He's awfully handsome," sighed Mollie.

Handsome? Peter? 'Course, he is. He's my brother.

Wednesday 31 July

The town was bombed again last night. The sky glowed red for hours, like a ghastly wound. Tip-and-run raiders, someone said grimly. The German planes nip across the Channel, drop their fearsome cargo and shoot off back home again before our fighters can catch up with them.

Shelters are being dug in the hospital grounds and there are sandbags piled up around all the buildings. We've got a guard, too. He's only got a stick – as we're a hospital, he's not allowed to have a gun. One man, armed only with a stick! How will that help us? At Dunkirk, the Germans blew up hospital ships in the Channel, so they won't take any notice of this, I feel sure. But then isn't this the *right* thing for us to do – and isn't that what this war is all about? It's no use – I cannot get this straight in my head.

In the afternoon I saw little specks appear in the sky again. I shielded my eyes to see them better, but they were too far away. Even when the drones got louder, I couldn't see the planes properly. I haven't seen a dogfight yet, but here in the hospital we see many of their victims.

Wednesday 7 August

Giles is dead! I feel simply terrible – but I can't cry. I learned what happened in a letter from his best friend at the station. They think that Giles was shot down over the sea. It happened on 23 July – that was the day I had my strange dream. For a long time I just sat and stared at the letter in my hand. I felt sick. In my heart I know it was a coincidence, but that doesn't help. Worse, I feel as if I let Giles down.

His friend said that Giles was a brave and gallant officer and that he knew he'd cared a lot about me. I wished he hadn't written that. Then he apologized for not writing sooner.

He apologized to *me*! I should be apologizing to him – and to Giles. Now I can't even do that. I didn't give Giles the support he needed. I never told him that I was proud of the part he took in rescuing the BEF at Dunkirk. I couldn't even be bothered to write.

Thursday 8 August

Jean found me in the linen store in floods of tears today. I couldn't talk, just waved the letter at her. She sat with me until I'd calmed down, and then we went for a walk together. She thinks I'm upset because I cared about Giles. I couldn't tell her the truth – I can't tell *anyone*. I didn't care about Giles, not in the way they all think. And they're being so sweet to me – especially Bunty. It makes me feel so guilty.

Sometimes I don't know what I'd do without my diary. At least *here* I can confess how I really feel.

Saturday 10 August

A plane was shot down over the town late yesterday afternoon. All the crew managed to bail out. One – the pilot – had gunshot wounds and was rushed into Theatre as soon as he arrived. The rear gunner broke his wrist trying to get out of the plane. No one was badly burned. We've heard terrible things – the enemy has begun bombing our airfields. Our pilots do their best to get the planes up into the air before they can be destroyed, but they can't always get them up in time, and runways and airbases are being badly damaged. If the enemy manages to do the job well enough, there'll be nothing to stop them from invading.

At night, the stretcher bearers rushed on to the ward again. Another plane had been shot down nearby. While another VAD made up the bed, I went to fill a hot-water bottle. When I came back she was expertly cutting off the pilot's uniform.

It was a German one.

I looked at the man on the stretcher. His face was very pale and he was sweating. He didn't look any different from any other young pilot. I thought I'd hate him, but I didn't.

I wrote to Giles's mother as soon as I came off duty this morning. After I'd sealed up the envelope, I burst into tears. I sat there, head in my arms, and I cried and cried. I thought about Giles – and about that German pilot. So many people's lives are being wrecked by this terrible war. Will it *ever* end?

Thursday 15 August

I was mooching around in the gardens yesterday afternoon when the Assistant Commandant marched up to me. Told me off for not having my tin hat and gas mask with me. "Nurse, what will you do if there's a raid?" She sounded really exasperated and I fled to fetch them. I'd just got to the door when Lieutenant Venables came out, still in his white coat. He didn't see me at first, even though I nearly walked right into him. Then he stopped, looked down at me and smiled. It was such a nice smile – as if he was pleased to see me, and suddenly I felt very pleased to see *him*. It seemed an age since I'd seen him – the day he stopped to mend my puncture.

I watched him lope off down the lawn and then he stopped and stared out to sea, shielding his eyes in the sunlight. I found myself wondering if *he'd* lost anyone close to him.

There was a raid today – a really big one we heard. We saw the planes fly over, so many of them. We heard the guns booming from the ships patrolling the coast.

I've had that dream again – I've had it again and again since Giles was killed. Giles's plane is flying seawards. A German fighter plane is on his tail. Then the pilot opens fire and Giles's plane spirals through the sky and bursts into flames as it hits the sea. All the time I'm screaming after him, "Look behind you! Look behind you!" It's no use. He never hears me. And the ending's always the same. The sea's always on fire.

Friday 30 August

My first day back on day duty – and such an exciting one too. Dr McIndoe was visiting the hospital! Bunty rushed over to tell me. She's working on the Surgical ward now.

I've heard a lot about this surgeon and what he can do for burns patients. We have a new treatment for burns now – our wards are full of men, their legs and arms encased in bags of saline. But this doctor can actually take skin from an unburnt part of a man's body and use it to rebuild the burnt part – their face or hands maybe.

At ten o'clock this morning the great man came. I liked his face at once. He didn't waste any time, but went straight over to the bed of one of our sickest patients, a badly burned airman, who was shot down over the Channel yesterday. Aircraft fuel supposedly burns its victims very rapidly. It's all to the good that he landed in the sea, apparently, as the salt water is good for burns, though you wouldn't think so from looking at this poor boy. We're hoping that the doctor will take him away to be treated at his special burns unit at the Queen Victoria hospital in East Grinstead. The poor airman can hardly move his lips but after Dr McIndoe had left his bedside and gone to speak to Matron, I could see real hope in his eyes for the first time.

Everyone here – even the MOs – talks about Dr McIndoe as if he were God. And I can understand why, if he really can help people like this poor pilot. He gives a burned man his life back – a far better one than he'd have without his help, anyway.

Saturday 14 September

I'm writing this sitting up in bed. I'm in a side room, off the main ward. My hands are still painful but I can write slowly now. Molly smuggled some sheets of writing paper into the ward when she came to see me earlier today. I didn't tell her or the others the reason I wanted them – to write my diary. Sister would have a fit if she saw me. But I must tell how I came to be lying here – a patient – while the memory is still fresh in my mind.

It happened nearly two weeks ago. I didn't feel particularly frightened when the air-raid alert sounded. Just weary. We'd had so many air-raid warnings before – all of them false.

It's always a frantic rush when the alert goes. This day it was no different. Off went our two newest VADs to the shelters, helping those patients able to walk. Sister, Bunty and I stayed behind to look after our other patients. Sister put up the blackout boards. This protects the patients from glass if the windows shatter. Bunty and I pulled the beds away from the walls and windows. We helped our patients put on their gas masks and tin hats, and then we put all those patients we could under their beds. The men always put a brave face on it, but I know that moving hurts them and I always hate doing this.

There were some patients we couldn't move, so we pulled mattresses up near their beds. In an attack these get heaved on top of the beds to protect the men from anything that might fall on them – like falling plaster or shattered glass. Then Bunty was sent off to look after a patient in one of the side rooms. Sister and I pulled on our tin hats and gas masks, too, and crawled under two of the empty beds.

High above us I heard the drone of the planes as they passed by. It sounded as though they were directly overhead. My heart was thumping. Would it be us this time? I was thinking over and over. Then I heard a single drone. It stopped. I saw Sister crawl out from under a bed, and I watched as she struggled to heave a mattress on top of our sickest patient.

In that instant I knew – it wasn't a false alarm.

Everything happened so fast after that. Almost at once there was an awful whistling noise and a huge crump. As soon as I dared I looked up. I gasped. There was an enormous gaping hole where one of the windows had been, and glass and plaster were sprayed all over the place.

It was quiet again. The barrage had stopped – for now. A huge cloud of choking dust billowed through the gaping hole into the room. I began to crawl out from under the bed, knocking my head as I did so. I knew I had to get the patients out.

Suddenly there was a screaming sound and the building shook again. I flung myself to the floor and felt the ground shake under me.

When the plaster and dust had settled I sat up again. There was a strange sort of ringing in my ears. I couldn't see Sister anywhere. I could barely see a thing through the dense dark smoke. And then I did see something – a flash of angry orange.

One of the beds was on fire.

There was a patient in that bed. My heart pounding I staggered to my feet. I grabbed some blankets and ran to the bed. No time to waste. Now I could see it clearly – an orange tongue curling round the foot of the bed. The flames leaped higher, grabbing at the mattress with greedy fingers. I flung the blankets on top of the flames. A sharp, searing pain shot up my hands and arms. I pressed down hard, smothering the flames under my hands, ignoring the groans from the bed and the pain in my hands. I kept doing it, again and again until I was sure that the fire was out. I looked at my patient – tiny smoky tendrils smouldered from the bedding. Hastily I pulled it off and wrapped him gently in another blanket.

I could hear sounds in the room now – as if people were moving around – but I could barely see anything at all as the cloud of dust swirled through the room and up to the doors.

Voices – my patients calling. "Jerry got us that time." Groans from other beds. Who else had been hurt? I had to get help – fast.

I felt my way towards the ward doors, calling to any patients who could to make their way out quickly. I felt pain leap up my hands again as I pushed open the doors. I wanted to cry out but I choked back my tears as I fell forward into the dark. A huge dirty cloud had swallowed up the corridor. I stood there for a minute, helplessly. I didn't know what to do. Then I remembered the side room. Bunty was in there. She'd help me. I felt my way along the corridor and into the little room. Every time I touched anything with my hands it hurt but I pressed on. I could hear voices – but they sounded muffled, as if they were far away.

In the side room, a window had been torn out, but there wasn't any other damage so far as I could tell.

Carefully I made my way over to the bed. I could see that our patient hadn't been hurt. I crouched down and peered underneath the bed. Bunty was still there, her head wrapped in her arms. As I reached in, I could feel her body shaking. I pulled at her arm. She didn't move.

"Bunty," I croaked through my mask. "Are you all right?" She didn't answer. "Bunty," I tried again, desperately. I saw her curl more tightly into herself. "Oh, Bunty," I said sadly.

Leaving her there, I stood up and made my way back into the main corridor. The voices I'd heard earlier were louder now. I leaned back against the wall and called. Through my mask my voice sounded so feeble. They'll *never* hear me, I thought despairingly.

"My patient," I heard my voice say dully, over and over. "Oh, please. Someone ... you've got to help him! He's been burnt."

And then there were all the others. Please! I felt someone pull at my arm. It hurt.

"It's all right, I've got you," a voice said gently. The voice sounded very familiar. And then I felt myself lifted up and all at once, like a curtain falling fast, darkness blotted everything out.

It was still dark when I woke, but now I was in bed and my hands and arms were in bags of saline and they hurt. I heard someone cry out – it seemed to be me. A nurse sitting next to my bed leaned close. "Are you all right?" she asked anxiously. I nodded, fighting back the tears that were trying to slide down my cheeks, biting my lips with the pain. I remembered all the burned airmen, and injured soldiers I'd nursed. Their injuries were much more serious than mine. They'd not cried, and neither would I.

Lots of people came to see me while I was in bed. Jean, of course, and Marjorie and Molly – even Sister Rook! The Commandant came too one day. They all made such a fuss of me – you'd think I'd be pleased but actually it was very embarrassing.

Then one day I heard the door open, and I looked up to see who it was this time. I was hoping it would be Bunty. She hadn't been to see me – not once. Marjorie had told me she felt too guilty, but I wanted to see her. I missed her.

It wasn't Bunty.

It was Matron!

"Well done, Nurse Langley," she said crisply. "We're all very proud of you." She told me that my quick response had saved a patient's life – probably several more lives, too. I asked her if Sister was all right. Matron just looked at me. I felt my lips tremble and for a while I couldn't speak. Then I told her what Sister had done. How she'd put her patients first. She was the heroine – not me.

"You were both very brave," said Matron quietly. "You're a credit to our profession."

She had a great many more things to say, but I can't write them down. I feel embarrassed just thinking about them. I don't think I've been particularly brave. I just happened to be there. Matron asked if I'd thought of training as a professional nurse. "You have the makings of a fine nurse," she said. She told me she'd write in support of any application I made.

I felt my heart swell inside my chest, and after she'd gone I had a bit of a cry – quietly, into my pillow.

I've had plenty of time to think about Matron's words, but I still haven't decided what to do. I don't know what I want – not yet.

Monday 16 September

It's getting easier to write now. Sister says I'll be allowed up tomorrow!

There was a tremendous air battle over southern Britain yesterday. I knew something big was happening – from my bed I could hear the drones of countless planes and then an angry barrage – our anti-aircraft guns answering back. Was I scared! I crossed my fingers and prayed we wouldn't be hit again.

In the evening there was another barrage – shouts and catcalls and cheers from the main ward. Sister popped in to tell me about it – a huge smile on her face. Later, the "up" patients came to tell me, too.

"Nurse, Jerry's on the run. Nurse, the RAF's clipped Jerry's wings. Hundreds and hundreds of Jerry's planes have been shot down." The enemy was bombing London

167

too, of course, but just then all anyone could think about was our victory in the skies.

In the end, Sister came in to shoo them away and the ward grew quiet again.

So much still depends on the RAF. If they carry on fighting like this, maybe the invasion will be delayed. Maybe it will never happen at all. Suddenly I found myself thinking about Giles. Whenever I think about our pilots I remember Giles and I feel so sad. And I know how much he'd have loved to be up there with them.

Saturday 21 September

I'm writing this on the train. I'm on my way home to convalesce – I'll be staying there until my hands and arms are completely better.

Earlier, Jean helped me pack my case. We were chatting and laughing together when I heard a knock on the door.

It was Bunty. Jean slipped out and left us together. It was the first time I'd seen Bunty since the day the bomb dropped.

"Molly told me you're going home today," she said.

I nodded.

"Can I do anything for you?" she asked. I could see she was trying not to look at my hands.

I shook my head. "It's all right, I can manage," I said. I hesitated. "They tell me that they'll soon be as good as new."

Bunty's face crumpled. "In spite of me," she whispered.

"Oh, Bunty, don't," I said, distressed. "It wasn't your fault."

I could see that she was making a big effort to pull herself together. My mind went back to another day, when I'd told her to take courage.

"I'm resigning," she said suddenly.

I was flabbergasted. "Why?" I asked at last.

Bunty turned and looked at me. "I failed you, and not just you, I failed everyone," she said. I was about to say something but she interrupted. "I'm just not cut out to be a nurse," she said. "I knew that long ago."

"Oh, Bunty," I said sadly.

"I . . . I just can't cope." She went over to the window and stared out of it.

"I'll miss you so much," I said miserably.

"Oh, Kitten," she said. "I'm so sorry I let you down." I couldn't see her face, but I knew that she was crying. I went over to her and put my hand on her shoulder. There were tears in my eyes, too. Then suddenly she stopped crying, and I saw the old Bunty in the smile she flashed at me. "What did Matron say?" she asked, almost mischievously.

"Oh, nothing much," I said, embarrassed.

"You're a good nurse," said Bunty. "Stick to it."

She stretched and turned to go, and then she turned back and we hugged each other tight.

I was dashing around later saying my farewells when I saw Lieutenant Venables. Was I better? he asked. In answer, I held out my hands. He looked at them for a long time. He'd been to see me when I was ill – not long after the air raid. I'd still been in shock and all I could remember was how pale his face had looked. Now I remembered something else. It was he who'd carried me away from the fire to safety. I couldn't even remember if I'd thanked him for it. I thanked him now. He looked rather embarrassed.

We walked outside together.

"What are you going to do when your hands are better?" he asked me.

"I don't know," I said.

And then he told me that he was leaving the hospital.

It was a shock. "Why?" I said. I was almost crying. I hoped he couldn't tell.

He said that he was going to work in one of the big London teaching hospitals. "They need all the help they can get now," he said grimly.

Suddenly I felt so frightened. German bombers attack the city nearly every night now.

"Why don't you come too?" he said suddenly. I felt something flutter in my chest. It felt odd but it was nice too.

"Why don't you?" he said again, seriously. "You could train as a nurse – a real one."

The fluttering stopped suddenly.

He didn't understand. To me, I was a real nurse already.

"Oh no," he said hastily, seeing the expression on my face. "You are a real nurse. I mean... You ... you're a marvellous nurse." He swallowed. "I just wondered – why don't you make nursing your career?" His eyes looked very blue.

"I don't know," I said again. I'd seen so much suffering already. Could I bear to make nursing my career?

I told him I'd think about it and then I watched him walk away, hands thrust deep in his pockets, white coat flapping in the warm September breeze. I was smiling. He'd given me his address. It was on a bit of paper in my pocket.

In the afternoon I was driven down to the station. As we left, I looked back at the hospital. The damage to the Surgical wing was being repaired. A lot of the patients had had to be evacuated, of course, but the damage wasn't as bad as had been feared. Soon, I feel sure, the hospital will be as good as new.

I stood on the platform, waiting for the train, my luggage heaped about me. I looked down at it, at the hockey stick and tennis racket propped against my case. I remembered the day I'd arrived. I'd felt like a schoolgirl then. I didn't now.

Just before the train was due a lorry screeched to a halt in the station forecourt. I heard the sound of boots as soldiers jumped down and ran on to the platform. A Sergeant saw me and saluted smartly.

As the train pulled up he was at my side in a jiffy. "We'll help you with that," he said. I wondered if he'd noticed my hands. I watched as the soldiers fought for the right to carry my luggage on to the train.

"Get a move on, lads," the Sergeant barked. He saluted again as I thanked him. "It's nothing, miss," he said. "We'd do anything for you nurses."

He turned quickly away. I looked at him, at the khaki-clad men hoisting themselves up on to the train, and then suddenly I didn't see them any more. I saw all those others – row upon row of wounded men – as clear as if I was still in the hospital. And I knew then what I was going to do. I was staying – here, where I was needed most.

"I'll be back," I promised as I clambered on to the train.

Historical note

In 1859 a Swiss businessman, Henry Dunant, stopped at the small Italian town of Castiglione. What he saw there horrified him. Not far away the Battle of Solferino had been fought, and the wounded lay in houses, and even churches, and on every street corner. French and Italian doctors went from man to man, working tirelessly, but it was clear to Henry Dunant how little they could do – and how much more could be done if things were better organized. So he stepped in to help. He organized the townspeople so that they worked together more efficiently to bring aid to the wounded. Even children were pressed in to help – fetching and carrying water for the thirsty men. And he made sure that *all* the wounded were looked after – even the enemy. And as more doctors were desperately needed he persuaded the authorities to release the Austrian doctors who'd been captured so that they, too, could help treat the wounded.

Henry Dunant never forgot what he saw at Castiglione. After he got home he worked hard to alert governments to the plight of the wounded. He wrote a book – *A Memory of Solferino* – and sent it to national governments and all the important people of the day. It described the awful suffering he'd seen but it also came up with an idea of how to relieve the suffering.

Dunant's idea was a novel one – to set up special relief societies, made up of volunteers, who would be trained in peacetime to care for the wounded in time of war. A committee was set up to look into Dunant's idea. Dunant, of course, was one of its members. The committee would later become the International Committee of the Red Cross.

Dunant knew that it was also very important that the wounded soldiers – and the doctors and nurses caring for them – be considered "neutral" in any conflict and thus protected from harm. Other governments agreed with his ideas, and in 1864 they signed an agreement that became known as the "Convention of Geneva for the amelioration of the condition of the wounded in armies in the field". The "Geneva Convention" was initially signed by 12 nations – Britain signing a year later, in 1865.

In 1863 the first relief society based on Dunant's ideas was founded. Many more relief societies followed – in both Europe and America. The societies adopted a symbol – a red cross on a white background. They would become known as Red Cross societies.

It wasn't until another war broke out – between the French and the Prussians – that there were calls in Britain for a relief society to be established, which would be based on the code of the Geneva Convention. So in 1870 the "British National Society for Aid to the Sick and Wounded in War" was founded. Florence Nightingale – whose work Henri Dunant much admired – lent her support to the new organization. Its first job was to aid wounded combatants – on both sides – in the Franco-Prussian War.

In 1905 the "British National Society for Aid to the Sick and Wounded in War" became the British Red Cross Society (BRCS) – part of the growing international Red Cross movement. Then, in 1908, the Territorial Army (TA) was created. Its job was to provide a military force for home defence in the event of invasion. The following year, the War Office proposed a Voluntary Aid Scheme. Under this scheme, the BRCS, the Order of St John (a much older relief society) and the Territorial Force Association were asked to provide trained personnel to supplement the TA's medical service. They did this by raising "Voluntary Aid Detachments" of men and women through their county branches. After training in first aid, members of the detachments – later to become known as "VADs" – worked in hospitals and dispensaries and at public events, developing the skills they would later need in wartime. As well as training in first aid, VAD nursing members had to do a course in home nursing. VADs could also choose to train in cookery, sanitation and hygiene.

Within a year of the start of the scheme there were more than 6,000 trained VADs. With the outbreak of war in 1914, many more flocked to join the relief organizations – about 57,000 men and women in nearly 2,000 Red Cross detachments. The BRCS and Order of St John decided to join forces for the duration of the War. They formed a Joint War Committee, enabling them to provide relief more efficiently to those who most needed it.

When the War began, many VADs worked in private homes that had been turned into auxiliary hospitals and convalescent homes. Then in 1915, owing to the shortage of nurses, the War Office allowed VADs to work in military hospitals. They were supervised by trained military nurses and worked under the hospital's Matron and Commanding Officer. At first VADs served in home hospitals, but as the War progressed more VADs were sent to serve abroad.

They worked in the newly established hospitals and hospital trains, rest centres and hostels for relatives of the wounded. But not all VADs were nurses. Some worked as ambulance drivers. Many VADs had enrolled as "general service" members, working as hospital wardmaids, storekeepers, telephonists, cooks, drivers, dispensers, X-ray assistants and clerks.

After the War ended in 1918 the League of Red Cross Societies was formed. Its object was to extend the role of Red Cross societies to other areas – like improving public health, preventing disease, and providing aid to people suffering from emergencies other than war – such as earthquakes and floods. The BRCS also established branches of the society in its overseas territories. The Junior Red Cross was founded for younger members. Welfare became an increasingly important aspect of Red Cross work.

VADs continued to be trained to serve in army hospitals, but now regulations were brought into force so that in future they could be mobilized to serve in naval and air-force hospitals as well, in conflicts anywhere in the world.

With the outbreak of the Second World War in 1939, the BRCS and Order of St John again came together to make the best use of their resources. Private homes were again opened as auxiliary hospitals and convalescent homes for the less seriously wounded in the forces. Initially just for officers, after the evacuation of Dunkirk many more were opened for "other ranks", and Rest Homes were established for foreign soldiers serving alongside the British. As well as serving in these hospitals and military hospitals, VADs also staffed first-aid posts, worked in emergency shelters, ambulance trains, hostels and nurseries. And a number served in military hospitals abroad.

When the War ended in 1945, the work of the BRCS and other Red Cross societies carried on. There was still a great deal for them to do. One consequence of the

War was the huge number of refugees and "displaced" people – all of whom needed help. So in 1949 the Fourth Geneva Convention was signed so that all these innocent victims of war were also entitled to receive aid from the relief societies.

But what of the VADs? After the War ended most VADs returned to their ordinary lives. But there was still a need for nursing members – even after the NHS was formed in 1948. In hospitals, Red Cross nursing auxiliaries worked alongside trained nurses, while other Red Cross volunteers took on other duties, like transporting convalescent patients home, or helping out at the National Blood Transfusion Service.

There are no VADs now, but their values live on in the work carried out today by organizations like the British Red Cross and the Order of St John. Over its long history the Red Cross has found many ways to provide voluntary relief to the sick and suffering worldwide. Its work continues to evolve. There are Red Cross branches all over Britain. Today you will find Red Cross volunteers doing all sorts of jobs – from fundraising and providing relief for victims of conflicts, emergencies and natural disasters – both at home and overseas – to tracing displaced persons and helping out at public events. If – at one of these events – you were to go up and ask one of these volunteers about their work, you may perhaps find that she was once a VAD. Maybe she will have a story or two to tell you about her work as a VAD when – as a young girl – she nursed the sick in the Second World War.

Timeline

1859 Swiss businessman Henry Dunant witnesses the suffering of wounded soldiers at the Battle of Solferino in Italy.

1862 Dunant publishes *A Memory of Solferino*.

1863 The Geneva committee set up to investigate the relief of the sick and wounded in war leads to the founding of the first Red Cross society.

1864 The first Geneva Convention is signed by 12 nations.

1865 Britain signs the Geneva Convention.

1870 The British National Society for Aid to the Sick and Wounded in War is founded.

1875 The Geneva Committee becomes the International Committee (of the Red Cross).

1882 The USA signs the Geneva Convention.

1905 The British National Society for Aid to the Sick and Wounded in War becomes the British Red Cross Society (BRCS) and receives its founding Charter in 1908. Its first president is Queen Alexandra.

1909 The War Office in Britain draws up a Voluntary Aid Scheme. As a result of this, "Voluntary Aid Detachments" are created by the BRCS and Order of St John. Detachment members – later to become known simply as "VADs" – train in peacetime in first aid and other skills so that they can help supplement the work of the medical services of the TA in war.

1910 The Voluntary Aid Scheme is introduced in Scotland. (Branches of the Red Cross are also gradually established in all parts of the United Kingdom and Northern Ireland.)

1912 A party of 12 VADs – the first to serve abroad – is sent to aid the wounded in the Balkan War.

1914 The First World War begins. The BRCS and the Christian-based Order of St John form a Joint War Committee.

1918 The First World War ends.

1919 The League of Red Cross Societies (now called the International Federation of Red Cross and Red Crescent Societies) is formed. One of its new aims is to relieve suffering from causes other than war. The BRCS establishes branches in British territories abroad.

1921 The BRCS creates the first United Kingdom blood-transfusion service.

1924 British Junior Red Cross is formed.

1929 The Third Geneva Convention provides rules for fair treatment of prisoners of war.

1939 The Second World War begins. In Britain a "Civil Nursing Reserve" is organized by the government to staff Emergency Medical Service (EMS) hospitals that would treat the large numbers of civilian casualties that were expected in the event of war. Owing to the shortage of available professional nurses, VADs are released to serve in the Reserve.

1945 The Second World War ends.

1949 The Fourth Geneva Convention allows for the relief of civilians in war, especially those in enemy territories or those living under an occupying power.

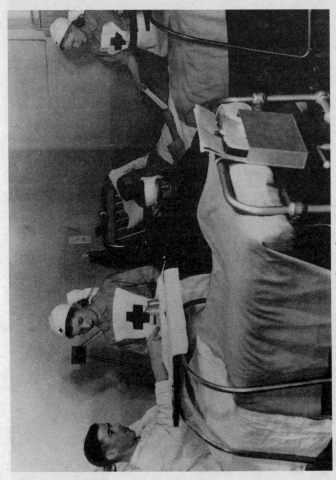

VADs working in a wartime hospital ward.

A wartime poster asking for donations for the Red Cross and
the order of St John.

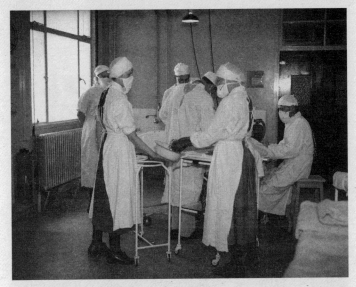

A military operating theatre in 1940.

Wounded soldiers arriving back in England after the Dunkirk evacuation.

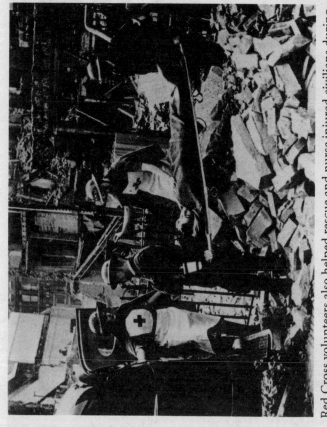

Red Cross volunteers also helped rescue and nurse injured civilians during the Second World War.

VADs dining in their wartime "mess". You can see the nurses' caps quite clearly in this picture. It must have been difficult to fold them properly.

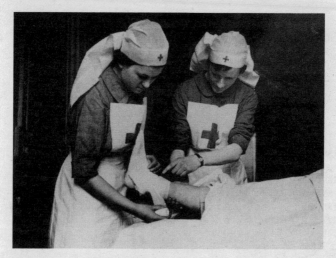

One nurse teaches another the right way to handle an ankle.

VAD nurses relaxing during their off-duty time.

Picture acknowledgments

P 183	British Red Cross Society Museum and Archives
P 184	British Red Cross Society Museum and Archives
P 185 (top)	Popperfoto
P 185 (bottom)	Topham Picturepoint
P 186	British Red Cross Society Museum and Archives
P 187	British Red Cross Society Museum and Archives
P 188	British Red Cross Society Museum and Archives

Thanks to the British Red Cross for permission to show the Red Cross emblem on the cover and inside photographs of this book.

Acknowledgments

A number of people and organizations have helped me with my research for this book. In particular I'd like to thank: the staff and volunteers of the British Red Cross Society and the Museum and Archive, Tate Greenhalgh (Thackray Museum), the Imperial War Museum Sound and Document archives, Kate Mason (Royal College of Nursing Archives), Tom Snowball, Captain Starling (AMS Museum).

My thanks also go to Jill Sawyer and Lisa Edwards at Scholastic for all their help and fine editing.

And to Jerry Crewe, Sheila Reid, Angela Sinclair and especially Madge Dobinson (Dobbie) – serving VADS in WWII – my most grateful thanks for sharing their knowledge and so many memories with me.